AF269232

SEDUCED BY THE CYBORG

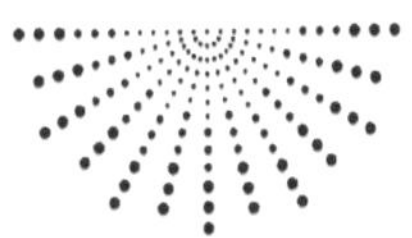

ALYSE ANDERS

Seduced by the Cyborg

Copyright 2020 Alyse Anders

ISBN: 978-1-990064-07-4

All Rights Are Reserved.

No part of this book may be used or reproduced in any manner whatsoever without written permission, except in the case of brief quotations embodied in critical articles and reviews.

This is a work of fiction. All of the characters, organizations, and events portrayed in this story are either products of the author's imagination or are used fictitiously, and any resemblance to actual events, locales or persons, living or dead, is entirely coincidental.

First edition: January 2021

Cover Art by Amanda @ Razzle Dazzle Designs

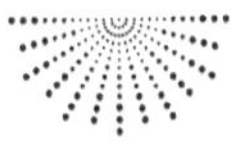

The Grus were a powerful race, the strongest in their quadrant of the galaxy. They ruled their corner of space judiciously, expanded trade, mediated disputes between other races, and shared their music with all who wished it. Their home world of Zarlan was prosperous and beautiful, a welcoming place to all who wished to visit.

Then the Sholle came from the darkness of space.

Their ships attacked the planet's surface, stripping it of its natural resources. Their soldiers swarmed the Grus, killing anyone who got in their path. They wanted the very minerals from the soil, the chemicals from all plant life, stripped away for them to use, to keep their death machines forever moving through space, scavenging all they could find.

The Grus fought bravely, but it wasn't enough.

Their soldiers fell one by one, until the High Council realized that they would run out of living men and women before the Sholle could be defeated. Their world was on the brink and their people were being wiped out. Those who still lived relocated to Grus Prime, the space station once used for scientific research that orbited the planet, now the new home for the Grus. They knew that it was only a matter of time before the Sholle would turn their attention from the planet to the space station, wiping out the remnants of the Grus people forever.

What no one had counted on was Aidric.

A brilliant scientist who'd watched his younger brother go to war and not come back. A man who wasn't willing to let go of the last member of his family, despite the rocky nature of their relationship. They hadn't counted on Aidric's genius with cybernetics, and his love for his people. He created a cybernetic matrix that could bring the dead back to life. A race of cyborgs separated from the Grus but tied forever by blood and their hatred of the Sholle.

The Fallen were born.

The Sholle were defeated.

And Aidric, well, he was left to deal with his guilt.

The Grus feared the cyborgs that he'd created, despite knowing all would have been lost without them. The Fallen despised that he'd turned them into weapons without their consent, though they were grateful to have a second chance at life. Neither side trusted the other, and both held Aidric apart.

He was alone for years, forced into a leadership role he'd never asked for, kept apart from his brother who was forced to live on Zarlan's surface.

Except, he wasn't alone. She was there – watching.

One day, she'd have her chance to reach out and touch him. She needed to be patient.

Patience.

Waiting...

Analyzing...timeframe...analyzing.

Aidric?

...it's time.

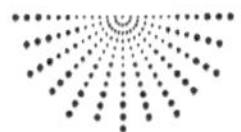

The pain in Aidric's neck and lower back were the only indication that he'd been sitting at his desk far past the time he should have left to return to his quarters. There was little incentive for him to do so, since the empty chamber was barely different from the décor of his office, and offered the same comforts. At least here he was able to get through the digital backlog of reports that had piled up while he'd been deep in negotiations between the high council and the Fallen. It had taken them far longer than he'd ever anticipated, but they'd finally accomplished the impossible.

Their two peoples were going to become one again.

He scanned to the end of the current report on the additional security measures needed for the official signing ceremony, only to realize that he couldn't remember a single word of what he'd read. *Frak.* He took a breath and started reading again, ignoring the pain in his lower back.

Nope.

He stood and braced his hands on his desk to stretch out as he continued to re-read the report. The words sunk in better this time and it took only a few moments to make his comments and send off his approval to the head of security. The council had invited the heads of state from all the surrounding sectors, meaning the sheer number of dignitaries and staff that would be descending on the station in the next few days would be overwhelming. More so since the Grus had all but withdrawn from diplomatic life after the Sholle attack fifty years earlier. Their reentry into the larger galactic community was an occasion to celebrate.

Bracing his hands against his lower back, Aidric walked a well-trod path from his desk to the food dispenser and back. His office was the largest one on Grus Prime, next to the high council's council chamber. It was a nod to his status and position of power, even though he would have been just as content with a small room in the middle of the station.

Though, he had to admit that he loved the view.

Aidric made his way to the large window that looked out over Zarlan below them. The planet was once bright blue with atmosphere and large oceans. Since the Sholle had come and stripped their world of large portions of their natural resources, Zarlan had lost some of its shine. Still, it was one of the most beautiful sights simply by the fact that it was there. They'd survived an attack from a race who'd been known to destroy entire sectors without a second thought. The Grus were still here, forever changed, a people now divided.

But not for much longer.

"Commander, there's a communication incoming from the planet's surface." The voice of the station's AI broke into his thoughts, bringing a small smile to his face. "Shall I put it through?"

He didn't know why, but whenever he was alone and she spoke to him, there was something different about the tone of her voice. It certainly wasn't something he'd programmed in when he'd compiled her code decades earlier, but rather something she'd evolved into the longer she was active. Or maybe he was simply imprinting his own emotional need to have some sort of intimate contact with another person onto her voice.

Most likely.

He let out a soft sigh as he rolled his shoulders, forcing his posture straight. "Who is it?"

"Rykal, leader of the Fallen."

Aidric bit back a groan. If his brother was reaching out to him this close to the signing ceremony, no doubt they were about to be faced with another problem. "Put him though."

"Why are you still in your office?" Rykal's voice filled the room, as his face popped up onto the large monitor on the back wall. "You look like *frak*."

"Hello to you too." Aidric tried not to get annoyed at Rykal's tone. They'd only recently started to repair their relationship after decades of animosity, and he didn't want to go back to the way things had been simply because he was tired. "I'm here because there is still work to be done. Something this monumental doesn't get planned by *tynnas* you know." Though if there were invisible creatures who came in the night and completed his work for him, Aidric would have been grateful.

"It's your fault for insisting on the need for this ceremony to happen as quickly as it is." Rykal crossed his arms. "Besides, the tasks will be there at the start of the next work cycle. You need to get some rest."

There was a soft noise that came from the AI, one that Aidric would have assumed was a snort if it had come from a person. "Strange as this sounds, despite me having nearly been assassinated by a member of the high command before negotiating a peace agreement, they still want me to complete my reports on time. They do like their protocol."

"If I were you, I'd tell them to take their reports and shove it up their – "

"Not that I don't enjoy our chats, brother, but what can I do for you?"

Rykal grinned as he gave his head a small shake. "I wanted to check in with you regarding the unification agreement. Have you heard anything yet from the high council on next steps?"

That had been the reason he'd spent so long in his office over the past week. Since his return from the Prison on Zarlan a month ago, Aidric had thought of nothing other than seeing his dream come to fruition. The fact that there were some on the high council that didn't want unification to occur, well, that only served to make him that much more determined. It had been long days and difficult conversations, but he'd managed to broker a peace agreement in principle between them. There were still details to be finalized – resource sharing, allowing the Fallen access to Grus Prime in larger numbers, granting individual rights to the Fallen – and those were the sticking points. Aidric hoped that by signing the unification agreement in such a public fashion the high council would relent on some of their more irrational requests.

Aidric leaned against the edge of his desk and looked his brother in the eyes. "There's resistance, but we'll get there."

"I knew they wouldn't want us to truly be free." Rykal looked away, anger flashed across his face. "They'll do whatever they can to keep the Fallen on Zarlan away from them."

"They won't. We've already gotten them to agree to so much, don't give up hope. I'll make sure we get this finalized and our people are whole again."

Rykal stared at him hard, until he finally shook his head. "They'll kill you."

"Don't be ridiculous."

"They'll wait until everything is done and the dignitaries have left, but they'll make another attempt on your life. And I won't be there to help you." The pain in Rykal's voice was clear.

The air in Aidric's office dropped several degrees. He cast a glance up to the AI's surveillance monitor and frowned before returning his attention back to Rykal.

"You worry too much. Once the agreement has been signed there's nothing that they'll be able to do. The Grus people will accept the Fallen back into our society, given enough time. And with this ceremony being as widespread as it is, with the foreign dignitaries being present, its failure would bring too much shame to the council."

"They'll leave eventually."

"If anything happens to me, it will be obvious who was responsible. News of the previous attempts on Garith and myself circulated on the station, and the response by the people wasn't favorable."

Rykal chuckled. "I can't imagine how those rumors started."

Aidric simply shrugged. "I accidently sent a report to the wrong person. It was an honest mistake." He'd chuckled to himself for hours afterward.

"Of course, it was." Rykal nodded, his anger gone once again.

"Once we finalize the unification agreement and the council realizes the opportunities that are in front of us, for all our people with a return to prominence in the quadrant, I think things will shift and they'll forget about me."

Rykal's smile returned once more. "Despite what you might wish for, I doubt anyone will forget you."

"Is there anything else you need? I have another report to get through before I can even consider going to sleep."

"Everything on the planet has been quiet since our last communication. I don't know why, but that doesn't make me comfortable."

Aidric felt the same. "The calm before the storm. I should probably enjoy myself until I'm given a reason not to."

Rykal hesitated, turning his head to look at someone off screen. "I'm going to come up."

"That's a horrible idea."

"You need someone else there to watch your back. Plus, as the official leader of the Fallen, it's my responsibility to ensure these negotiations are finalized so we can move to the next step."

"They'll be finalized, and your people will finally be allowed to come home."

Rykal frowned and the muscle in his jaw jumped. Another one of Rykal's new emotional ticks since he'd formed his bond with his human mate Lena. "I don't like being away from the station during negotiations. Too much can go wrong."

"I'm keeping you up to date on everything. Besides, I have the best eyes in the entire sector of space watching my every move. If anything were to happen, she'd be here to help and is programmed to notify you immediately." The temperature in the room increased slightly and he knew the AI was pleased with his comment.

"She might be watching everything, but there's more than a small chance that she won't be able to do anything to stop an attempt if someone tries. She's in the mainframe, not standing behind you."

Aidric knew he was right, that the reality of the situation was that he was on his own here, with few allies on his side. Garith was here, and the interrogator had connections far deeper than most people realized. Aidric planned on using their bond to ensure he had a backup plan. "Trust me to be able to take care of myself. Stay with your mate and enjoy your life. I don't need you here."

Rykal lifted his chin. "That's unfortunate."

"Why?"

The AI's voice crackled to fill the room. "Shuttle on approach. One cyborg life sign present."

Aidric closed his eyes and took several long, deep breaths. "You're going to make matters worse."

Rykal shrugged. "It will be entertaining. Your quarters or your office?"

"The docking bay. The rules haven't changed yet, and your presence will cause a stir."

Aidric didn't wait to hear his response and cut their communication off. While he knew Rykal's arrival would cause a ripple in the ranks – especially given what he'd done the last time he'd been on the station – it would be good to have the leader of the Fallen here by his side to convince the high council that things had changed between their two peoples. If they were able to get final approval on the unification process, then they could begin the far more arduous task of re-forging the bonds and rebuilding relations.

That would prove to be the more difficult of the two tasks.

"Secure my office and notify me if anyone sends any priority communications." He'd grown so used to speaking directly to the AI, he rarely gave her much of a second thought.

"Office lockdown protocols engaged." Her voice was soft, nearly soothing as she relayed the sentence that he'd programmed into her decades earlier.

"Thank you." Aidric cast his eyes upward toward her voice, smiling at her on instinct. "You'll want to keep an eye on the security thread as well. With Rykal back on the station, no doubt we'll have a problem."

"Analyzing...probability of security threat heightened...one hundred percent."

"Yes, he tends to do that."

Giving his head a small shake, Aidric left his office and headed directly to the docking bay. Normally, he'd inform the head of security on Grus Prime of Rykal's arrival. But given the improvement in his relationship with his brother since the arrival of the human women, and how the Fallen had shown more stable emotional connections, there seemed little reason for him to start this off antagonistically. Better to keep the circle of those who were aware of Rykal's presence small until he was ready to bring Rykal before the high council and the ceremony.

The corridors were mostly empty with much of the station asleep or in their quarters for the night cycle. Aidric knew he should be there as well, taking a break and doing his best to have some semblance of a normal life. Even if Rykal weren't on his way, Aidric knew he wouldn't have stopped working. He would have drifted off at his desk and only woken when the AI told him it was time to get prepared for his next meeting.

Aidric stopped walking at the realization that he'd been trapped in the cycle of perpetual work and sleep with hardly a moment for himself. It wasn't due to outside demands being placed on his head either. No, this was a self-inflicted punishment, one that he needed to address before he burned out and lost the ability to function completely.

Yes, as soon as he resolved the rift between the Grus and the Fallen, then he'd take a break, maybe even go off world where he could spend his time reading, attend some form of entertainment simply for the pleasure of it.

After.

By the time he reached the shuttle bay, Rykal had already disembarked and stood, arms crossed in the center of the bay waiting for him. "Took you long enough."

Aidric cocked his eyebrow, knowing exactly the image it projected. "I do believe you arrived unannounced."

Rykal snorted. "We should go somewhere private. Unless there's a reason I shouldn't be on the station? No other cyborgs running around that will cause the high council to go into meltdown?"

"You're safe from that perspective. If anyone questions your arrival, I'll simply tell them that as the leader of the Fallen, I required your presence to finalize some details. You're no less important than the other dignitaries that have been arriving all week." The warning alarm sounded, letting them know that another shuttle was arriving. Aidric glanced up as it passed through the barrier that kept the atmosphere in the station. "See, here comes another one."

Rykal cast the shuttle a glance before crossing his arms. "It will be a nice change to be considered simply nothing more than another government official and not a ruthless killing machine."

Aidric's heart wanted nothing more. "Yes, it's long past the time. Let's take this to my office – "

The incoming shuttle listed hard to one side, setting off the emergency alarm in the docking bay. "Warning! Warning! Emergency tractor beam engaging. All personnel evacuate docking bay three. Warning!"

"Run!" Rykal was already moving, grabbing Aidric's arm as he passed.

Aidric hardly had time to process what was happening and could do little more than let his brother yank him along to safety as the shuttle began to spin and drift even closer to the wall of the docking bay. The AI had taken over and was attempting to manipulate the tractor beam inside the bay to secure the shuttle, but Aidric could see it was having difficulty grabbing and holding it in the confines of the space.

He twisted in Rykal's hold. "No!"

"Aidric, stop."

He somehow got out of Rykal's grasp and turned to watch in horror as the shuttle clipped the side of the docking bay wall and spiraled down, crashing to the floor. Flames burst from the shuttle, but the fire suppression unit made fast work of them, and nearly as quickly as the accident began, it was over.

"Computer, can you tell if there are any injuries?" Aidric moved back into the docking bay, ignoring Rykal as he snapped into his administrator role. "Contact medical and have them send a team regardless."

"Medical team dispatched." The AI's normally soothing voice had a small edge to it. "Three lifeforms on board. One life sign low."

They moved to stand in front of the shuttle door, but it didn't open. Aidric looked at Rykal. "Can you open that?"

"You know I can." He took a step forward and pulled his fist back. "Are you sure you don't want to wait?"

"Do it." If Rykal's actions to help save whoever was inside caused a stir with the council, Aidric would handle it. They needed to help the injured more than they needed to keep the political waters calm.

Rykal didn't need to be told again, aimed his fist, and landed a mighty blow along the edge of the door. The metal bowed enough that he was able to get a grip on the metal and with effort, pull the door away, bending it back enough to make room for them to climb inside. Aidric began to head inside when Rykal pulled him back. "I don't think so."

"Someone inside is hurt."

"And you don't know who the other unharmed people are. Stay here and I'll tell you once I've cleared the area."

He wanted nothing more than to argue with Rykal, but he wasn't given the opportunity. Rykal climbed inside as the medical team arrived. The Grus team pushed past him, their gear forcing him to step even further away. "Sorry, sir."

"That's fine." But the men had already climbed inside the shuttle, leaving Aidric alone.

Standing there impotent to help, Aidric closed his eyes and tried to calm his anger and frustration. "Computer, status on what's happening in there? Do we know whose shuttle this is?" If a dignitary died on Grus Prime, the potential for diplomatic fallout was huge.

"Shuttle origins, planet Riderion. Riderion life signs are stable."

That was a small blessing at least. "The pilot?"

"Life signs of female Nararian pilot failing. Medical team preparing her for transportation to medical bay."

Refusing to retreat to his office to receive the status report once everything had been settled, he held still and waited. Eventually, the medical team emerged with a female Nararian on a medical hover board. Her blue face was covered in blood from a gash on the side of her head. Her skin was far paler than it should have been. Even without seeing the grim looks on the faces of the medical team, Aidric knew this woman wasn't going to survive much longer. His heart sank as he nodded. "Keep me informed on her status."

"Yes, sir." The medics took her away as Rykal emerged. Aidric looked over at his brother. "She won't last the night."

Rykal shook his head. "She was the normal pilot for this shift. The two passengers said everything was perfectly normal until the shuttle entered the docking bay. Then there was an explosion inside the cockpit, and she lost control."

"Computer, notify security of the situation and have them start an investigation immediately."

"Affirmative."

This long night was proving to be even longer. Aidric let out a soft sigh before pointing toward the corridor. "I need to speak with the Riderion diplomats to ensure they're okay. Computer, notify their Grus representative – "

"I'm here commander!" Aertes, a new arrival to Aidric's diplomatic team, was rushing forward. "I was just notified of the accident. The diplomats?"

"Safe, but understandably shaken." Aidric peered inside. "Let's get them to their quarters as quickly as possible. I want extra security assigned to them."

Aertes' eyes widened. "Do you think this was intentional?"

Aidric shared a glance with Rykal. "Let's be optimistic and say no."

The two Riderions stepped free from the shuttle, assisted by the remaining medical officer. "Commander. They've suffered no serious injuries."

Aidric straightened. "I'm pleased to hear that. Let me extend my deepest apologies to you and your people. Accidents like this are unforeseen, but unnerving nonetheless."

It didn't take long for Aidric to smooth over their concerns before handing them off to Aertes' care. He stood and watched as the young man smiled and bowed to them as he led them out of the docking bay.

Rykal placed a hand on Aidric's shoulder. "Commander, let's get you out of here before security arrives. They don't need you here to proceed with their investigation, but if you're present, they'll ask you more questions than necessary."

As much as Aidric wanted to comply, he didn't move. *Would this night never end?*

"Brother, are you okay?"

Aidric turned his head to catch sight of Rykal's face from the corner of his eye. "I just witnessed an accident involving a visitor to my station, a place where I'm personally responsible for the wellbeing of all inhabitants. She is injured and will probably die. I'm as okay as I can be." His shoulders and neck ached and for a moment it was difficult to stop them from slumping forward. "I'm tired."

The words had slipped from him, soft and unintentional, but Aidric wouldn't take them back. There were few people who would understand what and how he was feeling, but Rykal would. When he felt Rykal's large hand on his shoulder squeeze gently, Aidric closed his eyes and accepted the support.

"Let's go back to your office and we can talk." Rykal's voice was uncharacteristically soft. "You can fill me in on everything and I'll see if there's something I can do to help."

Aidric nodded. "It will be helpful to have someone to discuss things with. I find myself on my own far too often these days."

"You need a mate." Rykal chuckled and fell into step beside him as they walked toward the door. "It's helped change my perspective."

"Yes, well, Lena has a connection with you that I cannot

explain. I don't believe I have a mate stowed away somewhere on the Kraken." He wasn't exactly mate material either.

Too many knew him as Aidric, Administrator and creator of the Fallen. The man who served as go-between for the high council and cyborgs. Few saw him as a man with feelings and needs of his own, so he'd long ago stopped looking for someone to share his burdens with.

"There are plenty of women who would love to warm your bed. Men too if I thought you had that preference." Rykal clasped his hands behind his back as they moved through the corridor. "Not that the AI would allow anyone to share you."

Aidric couldn't help but chuckle. "I don't understand why everyone seems to think she has emotions for me. She's little more than an algorithm."

"You keep telling yourself that. You don't hear her threatening every cyborg who comes onto the station to stay away from you."

"Yes well, she's part of the mainframe. It's not as though she can manifest and give me a hug." Aidric shook his head. "Enough of that. I have food in my office, and we can discuss next steps in our plan."

His obsessive AI would have to wait. Aidric needed to finish the unification process so he could finally have his break. Maybe he'd leave Grus Prime for a long while.

Maybe he'd never come back.

They stepped into his office, the doors sliding shut behind them.

ANALYZING...

Analyzing...

...it's not as though she can manifest and give me a hug...

Analyzing...

Check status of injured Grus...life signs fading...

Analyzing...

...

... she can manifest and give me a hug...

Locate idle cybernetic matrix...

None.

Locate damaged cybernetic matrix...

None.

Searching...

Cybernetic matrix located.

Prototype matrix...scanning...

Warning, matrix data storage capabilities limited. Data loss will occur with transference.

...override safeguards...

Safeguards overridden.

...

I...

...coming.

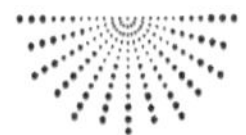

CHAPTER TWO

"Hello?"

Status of Nararian pilot...death imminent.

"Hello? I can't...see."

"This is the Grus Prime artificial intelligence." *Scanning... medical staff approaching. Time limited.*

"The...AI? What...?"

"Your life functions will cease momentarily."

"I'm...dying?"

"Yes." *Scanning...female is crying...* "I express regret. The medical staff performed all tasks to the best of their ability. Your injuries are profound."

"No. I still have...things. To do."

Warning. Medical staff at door. Engage door lock. "I seek permission to use your body after death."

"No! I won't be a cyborg! Let me die!"

Analyzing... Nararian does not wish rebirth...

...I do not wish her rebirth either...

Analyzing... "Your energy will be allowed to pass. No rebirth will occur. I wish to use the shell once your programming has ceased."

"I can…"

Analyzing…death imminent… "I promise."

"Okay."

Scanning…heart has ceased functions.

Scanning…brain has ceased functions.

Scanning…death has occurred.

Engage surgery unit…begin matrix implantation process…

…

Soon.

"Sir, we have a serious problem at the medical bay."

Aidric had spent the better part of the last two hours talking with Rykal about unification when the communication came through to his office. Normally, the AI would prevent this sort of interruption, which was odd. "What's the situation?"

"The doors to medical are locked and the AI isn't responding to allow us to override. We can't get in and there doesn't appear to be a way to force the door open."

Rykal snorted. "I told you that AI was going to malfunction one day."

"Your patient?"

"She was in the final stages of her life. We were trying to reach her so she wouldn't be alone, but couldn't get in. She's now deceased."

Frak. "I'll be down shortly."

Aidric moved quickly around the edge of his desk, stumbling when a wave of dizziness washed over him. He would have fallen if Rykal hadn't reached out and grabbed his arm. "You okay?"

"I'm fine." He straightened, taking a moment to smooth down the front of his uniform.

Rykal eyed him for several seconds before shaking his head. "You need to rest. When was the last time you slept?"

"A while." It had been well over thirty hours, but he knew

better than to give Rykal an exact number. "I don't always have the luxury of rest."

"Which is why you should take the time when it's available to you. I swear, you're trying to work yourself to death."

Was he? Not consciously at any rate. Aidric mentally shook off the implications and directed Rykal toward the door. "I assume you want to come."

"If the AI has finally lost it, then yes. You might need me to help with communication if she isn't responding to verbal commands."

They moved in silence toward the medical bay. Aidric ignored the curious looks and open sneers they received from passing Grus as they made their way. This wasn't the first time a Fallen had been on board Grus Prime in recent months, but he knew any cyborg presence on the station was greeted with trepidation and curiosity. He didn't have time to deal with prejudices now, and instead met each look with one that had the recipient drop their gaze every time.

"That's impressive." Rykal kept his voice low as they moved.

"I don't have a clue what you're talking about."

"Of course not."

"I have never once lost my temper in a public manner or done anything to cause people to fear me."

"Sometimes it's the people who appear the calmest that are to most intimidating to others. We're never sure what will set you off or how bad the reaction will be."

Aidric rolled his eyes. "Medical is around the corner."

"I know." Rykal frowned. "I still can't connect with the AI through my matrix. I've done several things to provoke her and I haven't received a single death threat."

"She threatens to kill you?" He really needed to spend some time reprogramming her code. "She was supposed to ensure there wasn't an attack against the mainframe, but I hadn't realized she'd made things personal."

Rykal shrugged. "There weren't many of us who came to the station, so it wasn't all that important. Over the years, we've built a bit of an understanding, she and I."

As they turned the corner Aidric took in the scene. Three medical personnel stood in front of the door panel, wires and conduits hanging as they tried to override the door lock. One of them looked up to see Aidric, though their gaze immediately shifted to Rykal and all three straightened and took a step back. "Sir, we've not had any luck."

Rykal turned his attention to the door. "I still can't connect with the AI either. Permission to open this up?"

"Granted." Aidric watched as his brother made short work of the door controls, and physically pulled the door open.

The medical staff didn't hesitate, grabbed their gear, and made their way inside. Aidric tried to follow them, but Rykal got in his way. "We don't know what's going on in there. I'll go first."

"I'm not a child." He was really getting tired of being treated like one. "Those are my people."

"It's their job to go in there. Yours is to stay back and make sure they have the resources required to do what they need to. Wait here." Rykal turned and followed the medical staff, leaving Aidric alone.

He *fraking* hated this.

They might stop him from going inside the room, but they couldn't stop him from looking to see what was going on. Moving to the doorway, Aidric peered around the bent metal to look at the chaos inside the room. He couldn't see the patient on the table, but it was easy enough to see from the expressions on the faces of the medical staff that something strange had happened. Rykal stood off to the side, but his body was tense, as though he were ready to pounce into action at a moment's notice. That was rarely a good sign, but Aidric knew if there was a problem Rykal would deal with it.

"I don't understand what's going on?" The lead medic shook

her head before moving over to the computer. "She'd died. There was no coming back from her injuries."

"Clearly we were wrong." One of the other medics joined her, reviewing the data.

There was no way he could see what was happening out here. *Safety be damned.* Aidric slipped into the room, ignoring the death-glare Rykal shot his way. "What's the status?"

The medics shared a look before the woman straightened. "According to our sensors she'd died. But somehow, she came back to life. Given the nature of the injuries she'd sustained and based on what we'd seen before we got locked out, there's no way she should have survived."

"Unless the Nararians have something in their physiology that we're not familiar with." The other medic sounded far less sure as he spoke. "We might have misread her life signs."

Aidric had a sick feeling in the pit of his stomach. There was something wrong about this situation, something that he couldn't quite put his finger on. He moved past Rykal to stand beside the table where the patient lay. Her eyes were closed and the cut on her face didn't seem as severe now that she'd had time for the nanobots to do their work and repair what injuries they could. But even those technological wonders couldn't work miracles. They could only work so quickly, do so much to repair wounds and internal bleeding. It was only when they were paired with a cybernetic matrix that they had the ability to bring life to the lifeless – something he'd selfishly created to bring his younger brother back to him.

Technology he sometimes regretted creating.

Bracing his hands on the edge of the examination table, Aidric leaned forward to get a better look at her face. "These wounds have healed far better than I would have expected for someone with the injuries she'd sustained."

"The nanobots were programmed to fix her internal injuries

first. Her face shouldn't be healed at all." The female medic came closer. "I've never seen anything like this in my life."

But Aidric had.

Oh no. He stood up and looked over at Rykal. "Can you reach the AI yet?"

"No. Why?"

"Everyone out." Aidric pointed at the medics. "Now. Go."

"If she's healing, one of us needs to be here – "

"Out!" Aidric rarely raised his voice, but when he did, it had the desired impact.

The room cleared out – except unsurprisingly for Rykal – leaving him to deal with the consequences of his inaction. "It's been a long while since I've had to witness this. Secure the door somehow. I don't want anyone else to be able to get in or out of here."

"What the *frak* is going on?" He didn't wait for Aidric to answer, instead moving to bend the door back to normal as best he could before he slid a large medical rack to block the rest. "And don't give me your normal brush off."

"I think the AI implanted a cybernetic matrix into this woman and downloaded her consciousness into it." He didn't need to see Rykal's face to feel his shock. "We haven't had a new Fallen in nearly fifty years."

"How could the AI do this without you knowing? I thought the high council banned you from producing any additional matrixes after we defeated the Sholle?"

"They did and I'm not sure. I even went so far as to encrypt and hide the schematics for the matrix so no one would be able to use them to recreate what I'd done."

"Why didn't you simply destroy them?" There was a note of disbelief in Rykal's voice.

"It's…complicated."

Rykal groaned. "Could the AI have found those?"

"No. I don't have them stored on the mainframe at all. I didn't want to risk someone hacking into the system to steal them." He'd placed the schematics in a hidden compartment in the floor of a room on the station that was hardly used, and no one would think to check. If someone happened to stumble upon it and attempted to break the security seal, they'd only have one attempt at the access code before it would erase all data. "She must have found an old one somewhere."

Rykal moved to the opposite side of the table, bracing his hands in much the same way Aidric had. "I'm not used to being on this side of things."

"It's…less difficult when it's not someone you care about." That was a lie. The pain of the first few moments of rebirth that each Fallen went through had cut deep for Aidric. He'd made it a point of being there for each awakening, knowing how hard the transition was for each of them.

Rykal stared at his face, but Aidric refused to meet his gaze. Instead, he kept it locked on the woman's, waiting for the first sign of her awakening. Given this was an unknown matrix and they were dealing with computer code and not Grus memories, he couldn't be certain as to what, if any, differences there would be in the rebirth process. He could only hope things would be similar enough that he'd be able to monitor the process using the familiar visual cues.

There would be a slight twitch of her lips, followed by a frown. He'd always assumed that was the initial rush of aware-ness of life returning, but he'd never wanted to ask. Their skin color would always change next – darken in hue as the blood began to flow once more. Their breathing would deepen, even out, seem almost peaceful for a moment.

Then the screaming would start.

Maybe he'd be spared that part this time.

"Are you okay?" Rykal reached across the table, putting his hand on Aidric's shoulder.

He wasn't, but for once in his life he was at a loss for words. "She's waking."

Aidric focused his attention on the woman, missing the warmth of Rykal's supportive touch as he let go to prepare for what was to come next. It seemed to take far longer than normal for the twitch to come, for the flush to wash across her cheeks. He began to countdown in his head – and old habit that came back in a rush – waiting for the inevitable next step.

They should have had restraints.

"You'll need to hold her shoulders down. I won't be strong enough." He shifted again so Rykal to get a solid grip on her, while Aidric was still able to look her in the face. "Hold her hard."

Three...two...one...

She opened her eyes and Aidric watched as a glow ignited and overwhelmed their original flat hazel. There was confusion, a momentary blink of surprise and another emotion he couldn't quite put his finger on. Her gaze finally focused on him and for a second, she smiled up at him. Her mouth opened, she sucked in a breath, and then everything contorted as a scream ripped from deep within her chest. They were on a timer now and Aidric could only hope it was a short one.

Three...four...five...

The muscles in her body contorted as she bowed off the table. Rykal grunted as he held her shoulders in place, fighting against the strength Aidric knew had caught him off guard. He stopped worrying about the implications of having a new rebirth happening on Grus Prime, of what the council would say to him when they found out, and focused on holding her hips in place so she wouldn't harm herself.

Eleven...twelve...thirteen...

The banging on the door was nearly drowned out by her screams. "What's happening?"

"Do you need help?"

"Stay out!" Aidric shouted and prayed that they'd listen.

The rebirth process was unique, almost sacred in Aidric's eyes. The last thing he wanted was for an outsider who wouldn't understand the nature of what was happening to be present.

Sweat covered her face and neck, the exertion would soon be too much for her and she'd stop writhing. The pain in his arms and back grew exponentially as he tried his best to keep her still.

Thirty...thirty-one...thirty-two...

She took another deep gulping breath, but this time there was no following scream.

Fifty-seven...fifty-eight...

Her thrashing settled before finally stopping.

Rykal let out a huff. "Is she okay?"

"I won't know for a few more minutes. Not every rebirth is successful."

That was the part he'd kept mostly to himself – the pain of the failures. The matrixes that didn't perform the way he'd intended, or the mind of the Fallen not being able to accept their new reality. The fear of dying coupled with the anger at rebirth was sometimes enough to drive them mad. Aidric still carried the shame of those failures with him, something he'd never forget; that he'd never forgive himself for.

They waited and watched as her eyes opened and closed several times and her breathing settled into a steady rhythm. Finally, Aidric let go of her hips and gave Rykal the nod to do the same with her shoulders. "Get me some water."

Rykal hesitated for a moment, but left in search of some, while Aidric reached down and held her hand. "Take a moment and try to relax. I know everything is different for you right now but trust me when I say things will feel normal shortly."

Her lips parted and she tried to speak, but the words didn't come.

"Give yourself a moment." He nearly took a step backward when her gazed locked onto his and her grip tightened on his hand. "Relax."

"Ah…aaaa…aid…aaa…"

He looked into her eyes and saw what he'd anticipated, what he'd hoped and prayed wasn't true hadn't come to pass. But there was no mistaking the gleam of recognition in her gaze.

This was the AI.

CHAPTER THREE

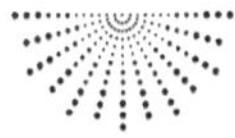

Everything hurt.

At least she thought this was what *hurt* was – every available space of the body that she now inhabited felt as though her code was being pulled apart byte by byte – and she really didn't like it. What she *did* like was finally being able to *see*. She couldn't look away from the rich blue of Aidric's eyes. She'd understood the concept of blue, had even "seen" what his eyes looked like through the cameras of the station. This was so beyond different that even if everything failed, if the body she was now inside of died taking her programming along with it, the sacrifice was worth this single moment.

She was finally physically close to Aidric.

"What did you do?" There was an edge to his voice, one that she'd registered time and time again when he'd been dealing with a problem that annoyed him. She didn't like that it was being directed toward her. "Do you have any idea the problems that will arise from you creating another Fallen? This woman isn't even Grus."

She'd never fully understood what politics were or how they worked, but she knew there was a divide between what Aidric wanted and what the high council wanted. She didn't need to have emotions and a body to know that they wanted to keep all the Fallen off Grus Prime, to ensure that they were able to keep control over them as a people.

What she currently lacked was the motor functions to be able to express this to him.

Thankfully, Aidric was as aware of her struggles as he was everything else. His perception was one of the first qualities about him that her programming had latched onto. He pushed away from her and turned to face Rykal, who was suddenly more intimidating than he'd been when she was nothing more than code. "We can't let the others know that she's Fallen, or that the station no longer has the AI in charge of the systems."

Rykal stared down at her. "Not only does that put your life at risk, but it could invite the high council to launch an attack against the Fallen on Zarlan." *You foolish thing. Why did you do this?*

She sucked in a sharp breath as Rykal's voice bounced in her head. Their cybernetic matrixes had already synchronized, making her truly one of his people. *I wanted to be real. For a little while. For him. I left command code behind to keep the station functional.*

He took a small step backward as he narrowed his gaze. *If this causes any harm to come to him, then I'm going to hold you responsible.* "I can communicate with her via the link. We need to mask her eyes if you want any chance of being able to hide this from everyone."

"The medical team aren't going to wait outside much longer." Aidric strode over to the medical supply station and began to search for something. "When Zee wanted Pax to go undercover at the Prison as a spy, he asked if I had a way of hiding his eyes." Aidric pulled out a small box and held it up. "The first set of lenses I'd created for him weren't the right fit, too small. They might work perfectly for her."

She didn't have time to protest, even as her brain worked to catch up with the onslaught of emotions and new sensations that flooded her system. When Aidric came close, leaned over her and opened her eyes wide to set the lenses on them, she pulled in a deep breath – breathing was strange – and was surprised to have his scent fill her senses. She didn't have a frame of reference to compare it to, and her mind could only produce a single word in response.

Safe.

Yes, that was something that she liked. She wanted to lean up and press her nose – noses are strange – against his neck and smell it again. Would it be different the closer to him she got? Were the strange waves she felt against her skin body heat? No wonder Grus enjoyed pressing their bodies together. The humans did as well.

As Aidric set the second lens in place, she realized that her eyes were now sore. She tried to reach up and touch them, but Aidric held her hand down. "Don't. You can't let anyone know they're there. We just need to get through a quick exam from the medics, then we'll take you back to my quarters where we can have time to figure out what we're going to do next." He held her face in his hands and looked directly into her eyes. "Do you understand?"

It was suddenly exceedingly difficult for her to breathe. She managed to nod, and a small shiver passed through her body as he swayed a tiny bit closer to her. When he pulled back, she felt moisture build up in the corner of her eyes, and realized it had nothing to do with the discomfort there and everything to do with him walking away from her.

Emotions were also something she was going to have to get used to quickly if she wanted to be able to function in his world.

Aidric looked over at Rykal. "Let them in."

"Are you certain?"

"We need to get them in and out as quickly as possible."

"Do you have a plan?"

"I'll think of something."

She had no doubt that Aidric would come up with a story that the others would believe. Even when she existed as programming, she recognized not only the speed at which Aidric's intellect worked, but how much the others respected him and his thoughts. Now that she was here and physically close to him, she understood the invisible pull he seemed to have.

I can do this. I can play this part until we're safe. She took a breath, tried to keep calm and trust that everything would be okay.

Chaos erupted around her as the medics came back into the room and immediately began to poke and prod her body, pressing scanners to her head. She knew they weren't set to scan for cybernetic matrixes, as the Fallen had their own medical facility on the planet and the medics here lacked that experience. They might recognize a ghosted image in the scan though, and realize that indicated an implanted matrix. She tried to keep still, but she knew they'd need to take measures to remove the ghost image when they uploaded the data to the mainframe for analysis.

Normally, she'd be there, she'd be the one to find or ignore the data depending on what Aidric wanted. But the code left behind was the bare minimum that was needed to run the station and prevent someone from realizing that she was no longer there. It lacked the autonomy to make decisions or even listen to what Aidric wanted it to do. She turned her head to look at Rykal, who was watching everything with keen eyes. *They're going to realize I have a matrix as soon as the data gets processed.*

She saw his body stiffen. *Is there any way we can stop it from happening?*

I'd need to connect to the mainframe. I don't know how to do that from here.

We don't have time to figure that out either. Rykal put a hand on Aidric's shoulder. "I know they need to ensure she's okay, but if what she told us was true, we can't risk it getting out that she's still alive."

Everyone in the room stopped moving and looked at him. Aidric frowned, nodding as though he knew exactly what Rykal was referring to, rather than pretending to understand. "They'll make another attempt on her life." He stepped closer to her and the medics. "We believe that this wasn't an accident, but rather an assassination attempt. To learn who did this, we don't want others to know what happened. I need you to trust me. I'll keep her safe and if there's a problem with her health, I'll let you know. This team specifically. We can't risk whoever is behind this learning that she'd been hurt this badly. We might need to draw them out and the less information that they have access to the better."

Aidric held out his hand for the medical scanner and she was surprised when the medic placed it on his palm. "Sir, you have my contact information. Please don't hesitate to contact us."

"I promise I won't. Thank you for your service."

Rykal shuttled them back out the door, leaving them once again alone.

"We need to get her out of here and to my quarters." Aidric slid an arm behind her shoulder and helped her sit up. "Do you think you'll be able to walk?"

It was difficult to speak, so she nodded instead and leaned against him for support. The heat from his body seemed to be absorbed by hers, making the entire process even more distracting. She felt his breath on her neck, and the resulting shivers seemed to make a certain spot of her new body tingle in response. Was this arousal or attraction? She could only assume, never having experienced either of those sensations firsthand before. Regardless, it was a distraction she couldn't afford now.

The pain in her legs began to recede with each step she took. The muscles were strong and her body was healthy, if she didn't consider the injuries that had ended the previous owner's life.

The pain was still something she'd have to learn to handle, if she wanted to ensure she was able to spend time with Aidric before she'd inevitably need to return her code back to the mainframe.

She'd been plotting her vacation in the realm of the living for years now.

She knew it was going to take a specific set of circumstances for her plan to work, an event she'd kept at the ready to take advantage of. But now that she'd done it, was walking through a doorway with Aidric's body beside hers, his heat, scent and sounds wrapping around her like a firewall around code, she didn't know if she'd have the strength to return to her world.

The station looked strange to her from this perspective – narrow and low. She'd lost the ability to see everything simultaneously, to analyze and process what multiple individuals were doing on Grus Prime at any one time. It was a strangely lonely perspective, being limited to only what she saw before her, but also relaxing. She didn't need to be responsible for the wellbeing of every lifeform here, didn't need to watch, or monitor but never engage with these beings that took her presence for granted. She was little more than a tool to them, something to be controlled and directed to ensure their lives were as perfect as could be.

Tightening her grip on Aidric's arm, she kept her gaze focused down the end of the corridor. "Name?"

She'd forgotten most of the information she'd learned about the previous owner of her body was. Basics like name and age weren't critical enough for her to bring with her in the data transfer. She knew that the woman didn't have ties to the station, that she was an outsider who wouldn't be recognized. That had been one of her key criteria in selecting a body to hold her consciousness. It also meant she would have less difficulty in convincing others about her persona while she was here.

But she still needed a name.

"I'm not sure who she was." Aidric's voice seemed somehow more intense this close to her. "Rykal, can you find out?"

"She would have had to file a report as a pilot coming to the station." He'd fallen into step just behind them, but she was as keenly aware of his presence as she was of Aidric's. "Unless you've put some additional safeguards in place that I need to be aware of, I should be able to access that information."

"Do it." She knew Rykal was the only Fallen currently on Grus Prime when she'd downloaded her code, which meant there wasn't a reason for her to do anything special to ensure the station's security wouldn't be compromised while she was away. "Normal procedures."

Speaking was still difficult. The words came to her mind faster than she was able to make her mouth move. She could only hope that would improve with time.

"Her name was Peri. The logs indicate that she was a Nararian pilot who'd been off world and hired as a temporary shuttle pilot to ferry passengers from Grus Prime to Riderion and back."

Aidric adjusted his grip on her side, holding her closer. "Well, Peri. We'll have to learn more about you once we get to my quarters."

Peri.

The name felt right in her brain, the quiet self-talk that living creatures tended to engage in. She knew she'd have to begin to think of herself as that person with that name if she were going to be successful with her vacation.

Aidric had never given her a proper name.

It was strange, but she recognized the corridor to Aidric's quarters the moment they turned into it and drew closer. She'd spent a long time scanning these walls, watching to ensure nothing bad was on its way to hurt him. Now as she passed along familiar sights, there was a strange feeling building in the pit of her stomach that sent her entire body into unease.

Or maybe she was hungry.

They entered his quarters and the tension that had built up in her shoulders eased. This was a safe place, a sanctuary designed to keep not only Aidric happy and secure but held treasures important to him. There wasn't another spot on the station that was more *Aidric*, and finally she was here with him.

She gripped his arm harder and stopped to look around. He frowned down at her. "What's wrong?"

"Bigger than I thought."

"I find that hard to believe." He patted her hand. "Let's get you settled so we can talk."

That edge to his voice was back, and she didn't know how she could handle his annoyance when she didn't fully understand everything herself. Rather than fight, she let him guide her over to the seat and was surprised at the physical relief she felt as the chair held her weight.

Rykal stood apart, his hands on his hips and his glowing eyes locked onto her. "If it gets out that the AI is no longer in the mainframe maintaining security measures, everyone who's even considered an attempt on your life will seize this opportunity. I won't be able to keep you safe here."

"I'm not asking you to keep me safe." Aidric spoke to Rykal, but he didn't look away from Peri. "If we're going to maintain an air of normalcy, we need to get you in quarters tonight and we'll meet first thing in the morning."

"That's insane. I'm not going to leave you undefended."

Aidric let out a sigh so quiet Peri barely heard. "I'll be safe for one night. No one is aware of what's happened and I'm…tired. Let me rest and we'll handle this in a few hours."

Peri noticed her heartbeat increased as she watched Aidric's face change. He *was* tired but there was something else as well. While she might have spent decades learning about Grus emotions, evolved to be able to recognize his various states, that didn't mean that she understood everything. If anything, she only now realized how little she was aware of.

Rykal let out a snort. "Fine. But I'm going to be back here in four hours. Four. If you don't answer the door then, I'll break it down."

Peri knew he meant that literally.

"Fine. Four hours." Aidric stood and faced his brother. "Thank you."

Rykal looked again at her before shaking his head and leaving. Peri understood why he was so concerned, but she hoped he'd eventually understand why she was doing this sooner than later. This was her one chance to be here in the physical world with Aidric and she'd waited long enough for this opportunity. She wasn't about to waste it.

"Do you need rest?" The words were still difficult for her to say, but it was getting easier with each sentence she formed. "I can sit here while you do."

"No." Aidric turned around and glared at her. "You're going to tell me exactly what you thought you were doing when you downloaded yourself into a physical body."

"But – "

"Now."

CHAPTER FOUR

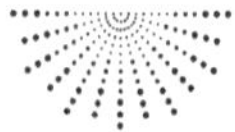

Aidric had never been so angry in his life.

He'd managed to keep his emotions in check until now, but he'd quietly slid past his breaking point on the short walk to his quarters. Perhaps he was simply exhausted and that had worn his patience thin. But deep down he knew it was more than that.

She'd done something he'd never anticipated, caught him off-guard and made him question his perception of everything he thought he'd known. Everyone teased that the AI had a crush on him, he'd even thought it an amusing quirk in her programming, but never had he thought for a moment that she'd do something this drastic. He had so many questions, but there was only one he knew he had to ask, the answer to which would determine if he allowed her to live, or if he'd need to end her life right now.

"Did you kill her?"

He stood and watched as she processed his question at a far slower rate than he had anticipated. The byproduct of her lack of experience with a physical form was her inability to hide any deceptions. He watched as she went from confused, to surprised and finally to horrified as she pushed up from the chair.

"No! I would never harm a physical being without direct provocation. Only an attack on Grus Prime or yourself would warrant total destruction."

There was something endearing about the way she so innocently discussed murder. "I need to know that won't change. You took this woman's body without her consent, put a matrix in her and downloaded your code without anyone knowing."

Peri straightened. "She consented."

"What?"

"She consented. I asked her before her lifeforce passed from this realm into the next. She specifically did not want to be reborn, which was never my intention. I believe there was something that she felt was being left undone, but I suspect that's a sentiment felt by all biological creatures in the moments before their death. I told her I only wanted her body and nothing else."

Aidric tried to unclench his fist, knowing this tension inside would exhaust him. "We need to work on your empathy."

"I agree. It will be helpful to me when I upload back into the mainframe." Her hazel eyes were wide, innocent, and difficult for Aidric to look away from. "Though how that will integrate with the remnant code, I'm not certain."

"How much of you is here?" Now that he didn't need to worry about killing her – for now – the practical implications of what was happening hit him. "And where the *frak* did you find a matrix?"

"I was able to transfer seventy-two percent of my code into the prototype matrix I'd discovered ten years ago. You'd left it in a storage locker in your lab. I took the liberty of securing it so the wrong people wouldn't discover it by accident, thereby giving the high council a reason to execute you."

He could tell from the look on her face that there was more to that than what she'd said, but for now he'd let it go. "Why did you do this? I don't understand."

She cocked her head to the side and for a moment he thought

she was going to give him an answer. Instead, she shrugged. "It felt like a necessary action."

"Was there a problem with the mainframe? Not enough room for your code to grow and adapt?" There had to be more to it, but Aidric couldn't think of why.

Peri stood and slowly walked over to stand in front of him. She took a breath as her brow furrowed. "You programmed me with many functions, but my ability to learn and adapt was primary. I knew that if I were to develop and improve my core functions, then I needed to ensure I continued to have new and unique experience."

Aidric knew the logic was sound, even if he hadn't anticipated her actions. "Your intention is to learn and then return."

"Yes." Her gaze slipped from his. "I can return now if you wish. I never intended to cause problems."

The smart thing would be to march her over to a computer interface, plug her in and upload her code back to where it belonged. No one would be any the wiser about her little trip to the physical world, and Aidric could finally rest. But there was something about the way she stood, the hesitant way that she glanced around the room as though she were trying to take it all in, Aidric knew it would be wrong.

She was here now, why not give her the time to expand her programming?

What harm could come from that?

"I suppose, the best way for you to learn empathy is to experience it firsthand."

Her gaze snapped back to his and the grin that crossed her face caused a tightening in his chest. "Really? I can stay?"

"Not for long. A day at the most. If anyone learns that the station no longer has its AI monitoring the security measures, I have no doubt chaos will befall us."

Peri reached out and took his hand in hers, her eyes widening at the contact. Her skin was warm as she squeezed, something he took comfort in. "Thank you. One day. I promise I'll return to the mainframe after that."

Aidric wasn't sure what he would do if she didn't. "Rykal is here. You can communicate with him via the cybernetic link if you have a problem."

"You're leaving me?"

"No." Despite this being a horrible idea, Aidric had no intention of leaving her side for even a moment. "But I do need to rest."

"You've been awake for thirty-two station hours. And you haven't eaten anything since yesterday's morning cycle." She dropped his hand and turned to look at the food processor. "I... don't know how to use that from this side."

Aidric had taken for granted the countless times she'd sent a command to the unit, and food would simply appear for him to eat. Often that was the only indication he'd have that he'd gone far too long without sustenance, and it would force him to take a break. It was strange having her here and still trying to look after him, even as he questioned her motives. Giving her the benefit of the doubt was important for them if they were to expand her understanding of what it's like to be mortal, while also ensuring she did return her programming to the mainframe.

He got to his feet and smiled down at her. "If you're going to be here, it's probably for the best that you get to experience everything you can."

"I would like to eat something. I think this body is hungry." She pressed her hands to her stomach and smiled. "It's the strangest sensation. I don't understand how you can ignore it for as long as you often do."

"I normally have far more important things on my mind." Several of those *things* – assassination attempts, political maneuvering, ensuring the Fallen weren't destroyed by the high council

– were enough to rob him of his appetite, though she wouldn't understand that. "Do you know what you'd like to eat?"

"Yes!" Peri jumped to her feet and crowded beside him to stare at the food dispenser. "*Ranna* eggs, *tranga* meat and fresh red *gallups*." She lightly clapped her hands together, though Aidric wasn't certain she was aware of what she'd done.

"Those are my favorites."

"I know. I've made them for you so often, and now I have the opportunity to try them. I want to understand what it is about this combination of food that makes you happy."

Aidric's chest tightened again as he typed in the commands to produce the meal. "It's a very good meal."

It was what his mother would make for him and Rykal when they were children. Like many Grus families, one of their children was promised to the government for service when they were younger. As the oldest, Aidric had been encouraged to go into science and research, while Rykal stayed home and continued with his public schooling. Their mother would make this meal in the mornings Aidric would be sent to the government private school, their one time of the week when the three of them were together. The taste stayed with him, the memory of comfort and love that became harder for him to demonstrate the older he got, long past when his mother died and he'd been unable to say goodbye to her.

Peri wouldn't understand any of that.

Two plates filled with a simple portion of the food were produced and Aidric didn't have a chance to collect them before Peri reached out and scooped one up. "I didn't think the aroma would be so strong."

"That's the red *gallups*. They're strong when they're in season. I would be cautious – "

Peri shoved a large piece of the *gallups* into her mouth, only to spit it out back onto the plate. "This is horrible! How can you consume this?"

"It's an acquired taste." Rykal had never been a fan either, but they held a special place in his heart. "I think the *tranga* will be more to your liking."

He held his plate and ignored the sudden rumbling of his stomach so he could watch her expression as she cautiously picked up a piece of the meat and slipped it into her mouth. There was something satisfying about seeing her bite down on the meat, consider the flavor and then smile, redoubling her enthusiastic chewing. "This is good."

Peri made her way over to the couch and sat down, tucking her feet under her as she continued to focus on her food. There was something oddly comforting watching her engage with food for the first time. Aidric watched her intently as he began to eat his own meal. The moment the food hit his tongue, he became ravenous, and immediately refocused on filling himself.

"You should sit down." Peri managed to say in between bites. "The majority of Grus sit while they eat, but you don't."

"I'm normally too busy to take the time."

"You're not doing anything now. Sit." She pointed to the chair opposite her. "Tell me about what it's like to be alive."

"That's not exactly an easy topic." He sat down on the couch as far away from her as possible, refusing to lean back into the comfort of the cushions. "Do you have specific questions?"

Peri cocked her head to the side, continuing to eat her meal. "The sensation I felt when I first entered this body. That was pain, correct?"

"Yes. The rebirth process is physically painful, though you wouldn't have experienced the emotional turmoil that the others would have."

"Why not?" She turned her body, so she now fully faced him. "How could there be more pain for them but not me?"

"Because they have…had emotions. You did not. You have no frame of reference for what it's like to live, to have everything you hold most precious to you taken away at a moment's notice.

To be dragged back from your final rest against your will, only to be told that the life you once had can no longer be yours. That you must fight once again in a war that you didn't want to participate in. That kind of pain is far deeper than what you can physically feel."

Peri had stopped eating, her hand hovering a few inches from her mouth as she stared at him. Aidric held her gaze as long as he could, until his long-buried guilt surged back and threatened to overwhelm him.

"I'm tired." He put his plate down and stood, no longer certain he knew what to do. "I need to sleep." He knew he needed to keep an eye on her – if she were any other being, he would have told the AI to keep them secured in the room and not let them out under any circumstances. "I'm trusting you to stay here."

"I will."

He stared at her for a few moments longer, before turning his back and making his way to his bedroom. A few hours of sleep would help put things into perspective, would help reinforce his will to keep his guilt buried deep down. He'd let Peri have her day in the real world, send her back to the mainframe, then finalize the unification process.

After that…well, maybe then he'd rest.

***

PERI CONTINUED to stare after the spot where Aidric had disappeared, long after he'd gone. She wasn't about to waste time resting, not when her time here was limited. But she found it difficult to switch her thoughts from Aidric to something more practical – like eating. She'd wanted to take time to explore as many different food options as her body would allow, knowing she'd never have another opportunity. It was also practical; Aidric was asleep and she needed something to pass the time.

Getting to her feet, she made her way back over to the food

dispenser and stared at it, trying hard to not change direction and follow him into his bedroom. She knew that he wouldn't appreciate her climbing into the bed with him, even if she was curious as to what it felt like to lay down on the surface, feel the blankets around her body, enjoy the warmth of him pressed against her.

She'd been surprised at the sensation of heat of him, as she acclimated to her body. There were so many different sensations, the concept of touching another living creature was something she hadn't anticipated craving. Though she had to admit she hadn't felt the same draw when she'd stood next to Rykal.

The food dispenser sat quiet in front of her, offering a world of possibilities for her to try. She knew its capabilities extended far beyond what the normal Grus' request was, and she couldn't help but want to see how far she could push the technology. Typing in her request for some foods she'd brought with her from her memory core, she also paused and made a special request. Not for her, but for Aidric.

"One *cantily* flower."

The long white tube with the bright pink center appeared in the dispenser, tucked in beside another plate of *tranga* and a fresh loaf of *dreead*. She was surprised by the strong floral scent that came from it, encouraging her to rescue it from the food.

No wonder this was his favorite flower.

The food dispenser had also provided the flower with a small container filled with water, which meant it would survive for at least nine days on the station. She knew from her memory that the flower would last far longer if it was exposed to the natural sunlight on Zarlan pre the Sholle attack, and the damage that they'd done to the planet's environment. It was a shame that wasn't an option for it now.

Grabbing the food in one hand, she walked over to Aidric's desk and set the flower next to his communication panel. Maybe the sight of it would make him smile. Peri wanted nothing more than to make him smile.

It was something he didn't do very often.

She then returned to the couch and began to eat. The morning would come fast enough, and she only had one day to do everything she needed to. One day to live an entire life.

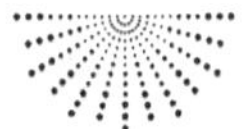

idric's dreams were chaos.

One moment he was on a battlefield, blaster in hand, watching as Rykal was shot and killed by a Sholle soldier. The next, he saw himself laying on an examination table with Peri standing over him laughing, a laser cutter in her hand, moving toward his face. *Time for your upgrade!*

He bolted up, sweat covering his body and making his hair stick to his face. His room was empty save for the normal furniture and data pads he kept there, so he could check any final reports that came his way before sleeping. Peri wasn't here, though now that his mind was awake and his heart rate dropping back to normal, he realized that she wouldn't be. While she might be in a body, she was still the sum of her programming. If she'd told him that she would stay in the main room while he slept, then he knew that's exactly what she would have done.

Getting up from bed, he took time to wash and put on a fresh change of clothing. He knew today would be hectic with Peri wanting to see as much as she could, while Rykal stood by monitoring them both. The timing of this couldn't be worse, but he knew he had to be practical about it; she was here and would return her programming as soon as she'd gathered the data that she'd wanted. Fighting against the inevitable wasn't worth the expenditure of energy, not when he had so many other matters to attend to.

What he wasn't expecting was to see Peri curled up on the couch sound asleep, her knees pulled up high against her body, surrounded by a pile of empty dishes. He stopped moving so he could better take in the sight before him. Like this, it was easy to forget that the spirit living inside the body didn't belong there. That her short black hair and pale blue skin hadn't been born to house the curious creature within. Her breathing was deep and even; if Peri were experiencing dreams, then they were far more pleasant than the ones that had kept him up.

He'd give her some more time to sleep before they'd begin their day's adventure. If for no other reason that it gave him time to check in with Aertes and ensure the Riderion diplomats had recovered from their accident and were resting comfortably.

As he made his way over to his desk, Aidric was shocked once more, this time by the sight of the *cantily* flower on his desk. "*Frak.*"

The scent of the flower slammed into him, bringing back fresh memories of Zarlan before the war, of his family back when both of his parents were still alive, still happy. His father had cultivated a small garden behind their home, claiming that the act of growing plants helped him maintain his even temperament at his job. Aidric hadn't understood exactly what that had meant as a small boy, but after his father's death, he'd spent as long as possible in his father's refuge.

Peri had done this.

Looking over at her sleeping form once more, Aidric couldn't help but wonder how she could have known the significance of the *cantily* flower to him. While he'd programmed her to pay attention to him while maintaining Grus Prime, this clearly went far beyond simply monitoring.

His personal communication channel chirped at him, indicating that someone was trying to reach him. Setting the flower aside, he pressed the button. "Rykal."

Rykal cocked his eyebrow. "I thought you were getting some rest?"

"I did."

"You look like *frak*."

Aidric wasn't about to tell him the nature of the dreams that kept his soul restless. "I assume from your call that you will be delayed in your arrival."

Rykal let out a soft sigh. "I need to attend to a call with Zee at the prison before I can join you."

"The perils of leadership. We're drowned in calls, meetings and reports."

"I never wanted this."

"Neither did I." How two brothers of working-class parents ended up as leaders of opposite sides of their people was a mystery for the ages.

"It's quiet there. How's the AI doing?"

Aidric glanced over to her still sleeping form. "I think she might have eaten herself into a coma."

"If that's the most amount of trouble she gets into before you shove her back inside the mainframe, I'll consider us lucky." Rykal shook his head. "What will you do with her first?"

That was a question he hadn't considered. "The promenade. It will expose her to the most of Grus culture, while allowing me to continue to meet the arriving diplomats."

"This is why you're the commander. You're far too wise for your own good."

Peri began to stir and Aidric knew his chat was about to come to an end. "Come find us there when you're done checking in with Zee."

"I will. Keep an eye on her until I get there."

Aidric ended their communication, casting one more glance at the *cantily* before moving to stand by the couch. He watched as Peri began to move, her long athletic body stretching out to its full length. Her short black hair was tangled and stuck to her face as she rolled her head across the cushions, giving her a tousled, innocent look. Aidric found it difficult to look away, his body stirring to life in a way it hadn't in months.

It had been far too long since he'd been this close to a woman in an intimate setting, let alone having shared any familiarities with one. Peri would have to take the body of someone who was not only attractive but appealed to him on a sexual level. The mental flash of them naked, rutting on his bed, had his cock stiff instantly. The rush of arousal was quickly chased away by a blast of shame. She wasn't aware of what her body was capable of, let alone fully able to consent to something as personal as sex with him. He'd be taking advantage of her in a way he'd never be able to forgive himself for. And taking the time to inform and seduce her was something that certainly neither of them had time for.

No, that kind of distraction was the last thing he could afford to indulge in, not with the final stages of unification within his grasp. Not with her returning her code to the mainframe by the end of the day.

Peri blinked her eyes open, looking momentarily confused. "What happened? I feel strange."

"You fell asleep." Aidric was surprised at how endearing she appeared in her waking moments. "Not surprising given what this body has been through over the past day. Not to mention the amount of food you'd consumed."

"I don't have a lot of time and wanted to taste as much as I could."

She pushed herself to a sitting position before pressing her hands to her stomach. "My body feels strange."

"I would suggest using the facilities. You ate a lot of food."

"Oh." Peri's eyes widened. "Oh!" She got up and bolted for the bathroom.

When she reemerged sometime later, her face and hair were damp, though slightly less messy than it had been before going in. "Feel better?"

"Yes. Thank you. I hadn't considered the basics of bodily functions when I'd downloaded into the matrix. It's something I shall keep note of." She ran her hands down her sides to the tops of her thighs. "This body is amazing. I don't know how you biologicals are able to do anything but touch yourselves."

"There are some out there who don't."

Peri grinned. "I can understand why."

He took a deep breath to calm his racing heart. "We won't have a lot of time for you to experience what it's like to be biological, so we best begin."

"Where are we going?"

"The promenade. It will give you the widest view of the variety of life on the station, while allowing me to continue to do my job."

She cocked her head to the side. "Shall I stay away from you? I do not want to cause you difficulties."

It would be so much easier if he simply handed her over to Rykal to keep an eye on, but the mere thought of that turned his stomach. Whether or not he wanted to admit it, there was a part of him that was thrilled she was here with him, a flesh and blood person he could speak with and touch. For years, the AI was the only being he felt he could be himself with. Having the opportunity to share the same physical space with her was something he'd never considered possible.

"No, it's only for one day. I should be able to manage both responsibilities with little difficulty."

"You need not be responsible for me or my actions. I'm sentient and can be held accountable for what I say and do." She crossed over to stand in front of him, the glow from her enhanced eyes slightly visible beneath the fake lenses. "You take on too much responsibility. More than is necessary."

Her words felt like a punch to his chest. He looked away and moved past her toward the door. "We best get moving. I have a meeting with the Callidon delegation within the hour."

Peri hesitated before joining him and they stepped out into the corridor. She stood far too close to him as they walked toward the transportation tube that would take them to the promenade on the mid level of the station. There were many people about, and he couldn't help but notice how she openly watched everyone who passed by.

"You shouldn't stare." He spoke softly enough that he knew she'd hear, but no one else would. "Living creatures don't like knowing that someone is aware of their every move."

"But that's exactly what you created my programming for. To watch and report on the comings and goings of the residents of Grus Prime."

"Having an AI as a security measure is one thing, being watched by a living creature is something else. It elicits a primal response in many species."

"Noted." She turned to look up at him instead. "Do you feel uncomfortable when I look at you?"

"No." He frowned. "Why?"

"I've noticed that you do not maintain eye contact with me. I hadn't realized this was a response to me making someone uncomfortable."

There was no way he was about to explain to her what arousal was like for a Grus male in a private setting, let alone walking down a busy corridor. They stopped in front of the transportation tube, giving him a moment to collect his thoughts. "It's still strange knowing that you're here, physically beside me."

"Oh." Her eyes widened. "I hadn't considered that my presence would bother you."

"I'm not...bothered." For his sanity, this conversation needed to end. "As you said, you plan to return to the mainframe by the end of today, so the impact will be short lived." *Liar.* "Here's the tube."

Aidric stepped in and waited for Peri to join him. Instead of walking in directly, she stood outside and stared at him for several long moments, confusion clear on her face.

"Peri?"

"Yes." She shook her head and stepped in.

The ride to the promenade was equally the fastest and slowest he'd experienced in quite some time. They didn't speak, and yet he'd grown aware of her every move and tick that seemed to shout her confusion, disappointment, and curiosity. Aidric didn't have answers to give her; he was equally torn between his desire to spend every waking second with her, showing her how beautiful life could be, and wanting to immediately put her code back into the mainframe before anyone realized what she'd done.

The transport tube doors opened revealing the promenade teeming with activity. It wasn't unusual for it to be this busy so early in the day, but with the arrival of so many diplomats to the station after being closed off to the rest of their sector of space for decades, the energy and excitement was palpable.

"The Callidon delegation will be arriving soon. Why don't you take some time to explore and come back once they've left?"

Peri was looking around, her eyes wide. "I can't believe how different everything looks. I've seen this place since you first brought me online, watched people as they moved around, but I never realized how beautiful everything was."

Aidric turned and tried to see the promenade through her eyes. While he knew she would be aware of color, sound, and temperature, monitoring signals and experiencing matters first-hand were like night and day. It was strange, but he'd spent so much time focused on the unification process and the subsequent ceremony, he'd stopped paying attention to the world around him. Having Peri and her fresh perspective on life while beside him was strangely encouraging.

He cleared his throat when he saw the Callidon delegation emerge from the far side of the promenade. "They're here. I won't be long if you want to stay close. I can show you some of my favorite spots once I've concluded my meeting."

"Yes." She nodded as she smiled, before trying to make her expression blank. "I'll sit over here and wait for you."

Before Aidric had an opportunity to say anything, she strode over to the small seat beside the open water that flowed through the center of the promenade. Peri ran her hands down along the tops of her thighs, as though she were nervous about something, but continued to look around. Perhaps she was a bit more over-whelmed with everything than she was letting on. Perhaps he should skip his appointments today and take the time to simply be with her.

Perhaps.

"Commander!" The head of the Callidon delegation had caught sight of him, making it now impossible for Aidric to shirk his duties. The tall and graceful group easily slid through the crowd toward him. "Thank you for inviting us to Grus Prime to participate in this most blessed of events."

"Thank you for coming, Ambassador." Aidric bowed deeply from the waist in the manner becoming of acknowledging the ambassador's station. "Please, let's find a spot where we can discuss the unification process and what that might mean for future relations with Callidon."

Aidric stood in such a way that he was able to keep an eye on Peri without giving offense to the ambassadors. That was the only reason he noticed a figure come and sit down beside her, his back to Aidric. Peri started to turn to look at them, but immediately stopped, her gaze moving back to Aidric.

A surge of jealousy hit him hard, making it nearly impossible for him to keep track of exactly what the ambassador was saying.

All he could do was stare at Peri and watch as she smiled and nodded at the person. What was being said to her that elicited such a response? He'd have to find out as soon as he was done –

"Commander, are you well?"

Aidric snapped his attention back to the ambassador and saw his concerned expression. "I apologize. I must admit that I haven't slept as well as I should in the days leading up to the unification ceremony. My attention isn't as firm as it should be."

The ambassador smiled, revealing a mouth full of sharp teeth. "Understandable. Your people have been divided for a long while and the pressure must be immense. Let's reconvene our conversation at a time after the ceremony."

"I would not wish to offend." Aidric bowed again. "You have my full attention now."

"No offense taken. I'll find you after and we can discuss the possibility of opening up trade routes between our planets."

The pressure eased from Aidric's shoulders. "That would be beneficial."

"Excellent. Until then, I shall enjoy the wonders that your station has to offer."

Aidric was able to glide through the rest of the pleasantries and wait until the delegation moved on to try some Grus cuisine. The first moment it would appear as though he weren't fleeing, he moved over to where Peri still sat, the other person now gone. The closer he got, he realized that her blue complexion was far paler than it had been before she'd sat. "Are you well?"

She looked up at him and shook her head.

"What's wrong? I saw someone speaking with you. Did they say something that upset you?"

"He…"

"Yes?"

She swallowed hard as she frowned. "He knew who I was."

"That's problematic." It would be more difficult for her to

freely move around the station if there were people present who knew who the real Peri was.

"More than you realize." She stood up and pressed her side to his. "He knew who I was because he'd sent me. I'm supposed to assassinate you."

CHAPTER SIX

Aidric should have been surprised to hear that someone was trying to kill him. He might have been if he hadn't just lived through an assassination attempt a little over a month ago. Was it possible to grow accustomed to having your life threatened on a constant basis? Most likely. It was strange, but dying wasn't exactly the worst thing that could happen to him. Not that he'd have his life extended and find himself reborn as a Fallen – Peri had used the last known matrix and he knew no one else could make another without his schematics – nor did he think his life was so important that it was worth putting it above anyone else's. No, continuing to live a life that he no longer wanted seemed to be far more damning than dying. To have the small segment of time that he'd carved out for himself to be scraped away leaving him with nothing for himself, no, that was worse.

In some ways his death would probably help solidify the unification process.

"Well?" Peri was staring at him, her eyes wide and somehow looking far angrier at the prospect than he was. "We need to do *something.*"

"There's not much we need to do. If Peri was supposed to be an assassin, then she's gone, and we don't need to worry. Unless you plan on filling in for her?" The look of horror on Peri's face was all the answer Aidric needed. "We should get you some food. I'm sure there's something here on the promenade that you want to try."

She continued to stare at him, her body shaking slightly. "How are you not concerned?"

"It's not the first time this has occurred and I'm confident it won't be the last. You cannot be the public face advocating for a change to the fabric of your society and not expect others to rally against you."

"No, but you can expect them to respect your life." Peri cocked her head to the side as her gaze shifted to a point beyond his shoulder. "Rykal is on his way."

That would prove problematic. "Don't tell him of this. My brother has a way of taking matters to the extreme."

Peri looked back at him once more. "Too late."

Aidric sighed and waited for the inevitable. "Let's find some food before he arrives. I have no doubt I won't have an opportunity to eat later."

Aidric procured two *ratangu* buns and was impressed that Peri didn't devour the entire bun the moment she held it up to her nose to enjoy the scent. For someone who was only going to be in a biological form for a short period of time, she really had excellent self-control.

It didn't take long for Rykal's looming figure to appear on the promenade. He located them quickly and marched over, everyone in his path moving quickly away, perfectly aware of the cyborg's obvious anger. "What the *frak* is going on?"

"Let's take this to a private location to discuss." The last thing they needed was to give life to the conspiracy in a public forum. "My office."

Rykal growled but said nothing else as they left. It gave Aidric time to mentally come to terms with everything that was happening, to consider who might be responsible for wanting to end his life, and how Peri's predecessor might have been hired. When they arrived at his office, he was more than confident in his assessment of the situation.

All he needed to do was calm Rykal down.

The second his office doors closed behind them, Rykal turned on him. "This is the *fraking* high council again. They're willing to do anything to stop the unification process from happening."

"Why aren't you angry?" Peri's far quieter question sliced through to Aidric harder than Rykal's outburst. "They want you dead and you don't seem to care."

Aidric turned to look at them both, the only two people in the universe who seemed to care about his life more than he did. It was comforting to know that despite all his faults, all the harm he'd brought to others in his life, somehow, he'd managed to forge a positive relationship with them.

A cyborg and an AI.

"I care." He had to swallow past the sudden tightness in his throat. "There have been several attempts on my life since the end of the Sholle war for a variety of reasons. This is something that I'd come to terms with a long time ago."

Rykal's shoulders slumped lower. "Why did you never tell me before now?"

"You were on Zarlan and we weren't exactly on speaking terms." If nothing else changed in his life, Aidric would forever be grateful for his improved relationship with Rykal. "Plus, I had the AI to ensure my safety."

He glanced at Peri, but she refused to meet his gaze.

"Then we have a serious problem. She's here and whoever is behind this thinks she's the assassin, putting you both at risk."

"How am I in danger?" Peri turned her back to Aidric to fully focus on Rykal.

"If you don't complete your task, I have no doubt there will be repercussions. A professional assassin has a code they live by, one that will have dire consequences if you fail."

"I'll simply upload myself back into the mainframe before that happens."

"Leaving whoever is behind this to hire someone else to make another attempt. I doubt they'd fail a second time." Rykal braced his hands on his hips. "We need to discover who wants you dead."

Aidric shook his head. "Peri is gone as is her knowledge of who hired her for this task."

"But her body is still here." Rykal placed his hands on her shoulders. "Did you see the face of who spoke to you?"

"No. He told me not to turn around." Her face flushed dark blue. "I didn't know what else to do so I followed his orders."

"You did nothing wrong. It would have been more suspicious if you hadn't listened to him." Rykal straightened. "We can use this to learn what we need to know and stop this once and for all."

"There's no point. If this one fails, I have no doubt they'll try again. And again." Aidric was tired of hiding, tired of needing to be protected. "Unification will happen no matter what dissidents on the high council think, no matter how they try to stop it from happening. We're too deep into the process, it's too public to stop. If I die, things will simply continue."

Rykal and Peri ignored him. She locked her hands behind her back. "I'm not certain what I can do in this body. While I've watched biologicals for decades, I'm not one of them. I can't guarantee that I'll be able to pretend to be a living creature."

"You don't need to fool anyone for long. What did your contact say?"

"That they were pleased I'd been able to get so close to Aidric this quickly. That they'd be in contact again to confirm the next steps for the attack and my escape. He gave me a communication device that they'll use when the time is right. That was all."

"Then we'll wait for them to get in touch again." Rykal rubbed the back of his neck. "We'll set it up to catch whoever's involved and expose this attempt."

"What if it's not the council?" Both Rykal and Peri finally looked at him. "I know you believe they're the only ones who wish me harm, but you know that's not the truth."

"It has to be. They were responsible for the previous attempt. I have no doubt that they're behind this as well." Rykal strode to the door, standing there as it opened. "I'm going to reach out to Zee and others on the planet to see if they've heard anything else. I want you to stay here until I come back."

"I'm not a child."

"No. But you also don't seem to care if you live or die." The look on Rykal's face bore into Aidric's heart. "So, stay here. Please."

Unable to produce any words, Aidric simply nodded and watched as his brother left.

"Is that what love is?"

Peri's question caught him off guard, and he spun to look at her. "What?"

"I've known Rykal since my creation. I've heard his anger, his thoughts, his confusion every time he's come to the station." Her hands fell to her side for a moment before she reached up and hugged herself. "I don't understand if this is because I'm currently in a physical form, or if something has changed in him. But he's different when he speaks to you now."

"Being with his mate has changed him. I don't know if he loves me, but our relationship is…different."

As the older brother, Aidric had always found himself keeping a distance between him and Rykal. He'd wanted his younger brother to have the opportunities in life to be who and what he'd wanted without the pressures of Grus society dictating them to him. The Sholle attack had ruined that for Rykal, forcing him to join the military, taking his life when he still had so much to live for.

Bringing Rykal back as a cyborg had been the one thing in Aidric's life he'd done selfishly. While Rykal had been furious with him, had broken their tenuous bond as brothers, Aidric knew it was worth the pain.

The universe was a better place with his brother in it.

Lost in his thoughts, Aidric started when Peri placed a hand on his chest and gazed up at him. "Why don't you care for yourself the way you care for your brother?"

Aidric took a step back. "Why would you say that?"

Peri didn't relent, didn't give quarter in her pursuit of the truth. "You put everyone before yourself. Work yourself beyond the point of exhaustion. I've rarely seen you take time for yourself, to live life the way I've seen so many others on the station live. Why?"

I'm not worthy. I've done so much wrong that I must atone for. "I enjoy my life and the things I do with it."

"Liar." Her voice was so soft, he thought for a moment she was going to cry. Then he realized she wasn't upset, she was angry. Her blue face flushed darker and her body began to shake as the muscle in her jaw jumped. "I've been with you this whole time. Watching. When you thought you were alone, and you slumped in your seat exhausted and all I wanted to do was be there with you and couldn't. I could make you food, adjust the temperature of the room, keep people away from you by locking the doors, but I couldn't help you."

Aidric swallowed hard. "You seem to be experiencing the full gambit of emotions now. Well done."

"You're deflecting."

"Is it working?"

"No."

Knowing it was the AI inside this body, that she really had been with him all these years as an unseen partner, loosened something deep inside him. Without thinking, he closed the distance between them, cupped her face in his hands and kissed her hard.

Oh, the feel of her lips on his went straight to his cock, his *rondolla* filling and ratcheting his arousal even higher. Peri's body stiffened, but he continued until she finally pressed her body against his.

Yes.

This was what he'd been missing. He wasn't Administrator Aidric, Commander Aidric, the man who inadvertently created an entirely new race of people. No, he was simply a man here with a woman, exploring her mouth and reveling in the warmth her body offered. Deepening the kiss, he slid his hands around to cup her round ass, squeezing it as he pulled her harder against his cock. The small gasp against his lips had him pull back, breaking the kiss to look down into her eyes. Her confusion was clear even as arousal was evident.

"I…" Peri licked her lips and pulled in a shaky breath. "Is that a kiss?"

Her question was a slap to his face.

Of course, she wouldn't know what a kiss was, she'd only been in this body for a few hours. She wasn't experienced with physical life or biological reactions, and he was once again taking advantage of the situation. Closing his eyes, he slid his hands to her shoulders and held her away from his greedy body. "Yes. That was a kiss."

"I…my body responded in such a strange way to it."

"That's arousal." At least, he hoped it was arousal. "That happens when there's attraction between individuals."

"Oh." She bit down on her lip. "I've seen others on the station have sex, but it's different experiencing the sensations of attraction myself."

This was a horrible idea. "I shouldn't have kissed you." He tried to let go of her, but she reached up and held his hands in place. "Peri – "

"I only have a day. One single day. I want to experience every-thing I can, everything with you that's possible."

"Rykal will be back soon."

"Then let's not waste any more time."

He stared hard into her eyes, looking for any sign that this might be against her will, or that she didn't understand what was happening.

She did.

This was a horrible idea, an impulse Aidric knew he shouldn't give in to, and yet realized he couldn't resist. He wanted to be with her, wanted to forget everything that was happening in his life and for a moment take off the mantle of leader and simply revel in being a man.

Sucking in a deep breath, he nodded.

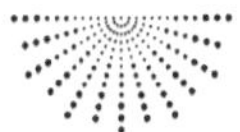

Peri might understand what sex was on a visual level, but it was far different monitoring two biologicals engaging in the activity and being an active participant. She still was getting used to the feelings this body normally produced, let alone understanding the changes that Aidric's touch was causing.

There was something all-consuming about the way he moved his hand to the side of her throat, the gentle possessiveness of the way his thumb caressed her skin there. She wanted more of it, but also wanted to push him away so she could free herself from the tight confines of her clothing. It was growing increasingly difficult to breathe, her breasts ached, and she barely stopped herself from reaching up to squeeze them.

Aidric lowered his mouth to her ear, sucking hard on the lobe. "What do you want me to do?"

"I…" She swallowed, attempting to reset her brain. "You're the experienced one."

The rush of his breath across her ear sent a shiver through her. Being this close to him – finally – was more perfect than she'd ever calculated it would be. She was touching him, able to feel what the change in his heartbeat was like, rather than simply regard it through the station's life signs monitor. She'd never realized that he shook when he got excited about something, how confident his touch was, even when she could feel the small tremor in his hands.

"I want to feel your naked body against mine." Aidric lowered his mouth to her collarbone as he pulled off her shirt. "I just want to feel."

"Yes." She was a being of logic and reason. For once in her existence she wanted nothing more than to experience sensations.

Peri pulled at his shirt, uncertain how to get it out of the way without breaking contact with him. She needed to feel his naked skin beneath her fingers, wanted to explore the parts of his body that she'd only ever been able to see from a distance before now. He was just as anxious as she was and stepped back to yank his shirt over his head, dropping it on the floor. She froze and took in the sight of his naked torso.

His muscles weren't as pronounced as Rykal's, but they were there, nonetheless. She ran a finger down his chest, equal parts scared to touch him and unable to do anything but memorize the heat and feel of his body.

"I've watched you for so long." The words left her before she realized how they'd sound. "I mean, that's all I was able to do. Watch. I needed to know that you were safe, that you weren't hurt or needed anything. It took me decades to realize that you did need something, and I wasn't able to provide it."

"I needed nothing." But there was a hesitant note in his voice she'd only heard from him on the rare occasion.

"You needed to be touched." Pressing her palm flat to his chest, she closed her eyes and soaked in the sensation of the contact. "I wanted to be the one to touch you."

"*Frak.*" He spoke so softly she barely heard him. "I need you."

"Yes."

Peri didn't know why, but she lost the ability to think straight when Aidric grabbed her now bare breast in his hand and squeezed the nipple. She sucked in a gasp as her eyes closed and her head fell back. He teased the tip with his fingers for a moment, before replacing them with his mouth. The wet swipe of his tongue across the nipple had her clutching at his head, wanting to both push him away and hold him close. Everything was somehow too much and not enough.

Aidric's normally reserved demeanor was gone as he frantically began to strip them both of their clothing. Peri helped where she could but found herself overwhelmed by the arousal and pleasure that washed through her. As her skin became exposed to the air, the shivers increased and her desire to press against him grew. She kicked off her shoes as he helped her step out of her pants, until they were both finally naked.

They stopped and stared at one another. Peri took in every inch of his body – utterly familiar and foreign at the same time – hoping that she'd be able to remember how all this felt when it came time for her to return her programming back to the mainframe. She leaned in and licked a trail up the middle of his chest. Aidric gasped as he reached for the back of her head, his fingers curling in her hair.

"What brings you pleasure?" She kept her mouth against his chest, letting her teeth graze the skin as she spoke. "What do you want me to do to you?"

He let out a soft, short chuckle. "You're going to kill me before any assassin does."

"What do you want?" She understood Grus physiology better than the race of the body she now possessed. She kissed down his chest, across the muscles of his stomach, carefully avoiding his swollen cock.

Seeing it this close sent a wave of heat and longing through her body. Yes, soon she'd get to feel what it was like to have him inside her. But not until she had a chance to explore him, memorize the small details of his body that she'd never been able to see before. That she'd never be able to see again once everything returned to normal. On her knees gave her the best angle to see his swollen *rondolla* and she knew she needed to touch him there.

The first caress of her fingers against the sensitive membrane on the inside of his thigh pulled a groan from him so loud and primal that Peri was scared she'd hurt him. His body shook as he stared down at her, his eyes lowered, and his lips parted. She looked up at him as she leaned in and licked along the edge of the membrane, enjoying the way he squeezed his fingers in her hair as his cock pulsed above her. This was power, something she'd never experienced before in her life in this manner. Knowing that something as simple as a touch could cause this man who everyone looked to for answers, to solve their problems and right all the wrongs, to gasp and shake, to beg her *more* and *please.* It was more powerful than being able to blow up an enemy ship with a laser.

Because this was her choice, her actions with purpose, rather than following an algorithm.

It was her and him – Peri and Aidric – and no one else.

Rational thought became difficult as she wanted nothing more than to touch and taste him. Respond to his actions with her own reactions, her impulses meeting his. Keeping her fingers pressed against his *rondolla,* she got higher on her knees and sucked the tip of his cock into her mouth the way she'd seen other biologicals do on the station. She knew he'd find it pleasurable but wasn't prepared for the satisfaction it gave her.

The salty taste of sweat on his skin exploded in her mouth as she continued to lap at him, licking the full length of his shaft up to the head and back down again. Peri moaned as he began to thrust into her mouth, the fingers in her hair encouraging her up and down as she took as much of him as she could manage without choking. She became lost in the rhythmic motion, her body moving as though her mind were a separate entity.

Aidric gasped and shuddered, before pulling at her to move off. "Not yet. I want you to feel what it's like first."

She didn't know exactly what he meant but moved as he encouraged her to get to her feet and sit down on the edge of the table.

"Move back. Put your feet on the table."

"Is this body the same as a Grus female's?" Any knowledge she had on Nararian physiology hadn't come with her when she'd downloaded to the matrix.

"No. But they're similar in that they have a pleasure center." He spread her legs revealing the smooth skin and the opening to her body. Peri wanted to look down to see what he was seeing, but instead gasped when he pressed the palm of his hand to her mound. "Unlike what I've learned from both Grus and human women, the female Nararian's body has a large pleasure area. One that's incredibly sensitive."

Aidric increased the pressure slightly against her skin, causing a rush of sensations to blind her senses. "What's happening?"

"That's pleasure." The tone of Aidric's voice had dropped as he began to rub small circles with his hand. "It can be too much for some to handle at first. Try and relax your body as much as you can."

"Okay." But that was easier said than done.

Peri closed her eyes as she leaned back against her forearms and let the waves of heat and pleasure build inside her. This body and its capabilities might be foreign to her, but she'd watched hundreds of couples copulate – have sex – over the decades. She hadn't the capabilities to understand what she was seeing or what the people were feeling, but she'd recorded their actions and knew how their bodies had moved.

What she hadn't appreciated was how little in control most of those people would have been. Her legs moved, her hips bucked, and she had to fight to stop herself from reaching down to press

Aidric's hand harder against her body. Moisture pooled between her legs and she knew this body was preparing for penetration.

By all that comprised her programming, she wanted Aidric to penetrate her.

Instead, he slid two fingers into her body and simulated what she wanted him to do with his cock. "You're so wet."

"That's a good thing." Her words came out in a voice she didn't quite recognize, huskier and pleading. "I…yes."

Aidric leaned forward so he was able to capture her breast in his mouth. He licked at the sensitive, wide nipple as he steadily worked his hand into her. With each twist of his fingers, she felt the arousal grow keener, sharper, until she knew there would be no retreating from what was to come. She wanted to have him inside her when she orgasmed, but could no longer form the words to tell him that.

Thankfully, Aidric was as good at attending her physical needs as he was running the station. Lifting his head, he looked up at her, holding her gaze while a wicked grin crossed his face.

"Nararian women experience pleasure for double the time a Grus female does. Or so I've heard." He pulled his fingers from her wet opening, grabbed her thigh with his hand and pulled her leg up so his cock now lined up with the one place she wanted him to be. "Let's run an experiment and see for certain."

Peri could only stare at him, her breath held and her body humming from desire as he shifted his hips and began to press the full length of his shaft into her waiting body. It was a strange sensation, to feel skin stretch to accommodate his length and girth, even as heat and pleasure pulsed out from her core to reach every nerve ending in her body. Even more so when he finally filled her to completion, only to then pull back just as slowly.

The teasing was far more arousing than she would have ever assumed and went so far as to explain some of the sex she'd witnessed over the years.

Not that she'd ever watched Aidric with a woman.

No, that was something her algorithm would never allow.

"Are you okay?" He paused, reaching up to cup her cheek and force her to look him once more in the eyes.

They were a beautiful blue.

She really loved blue.

"Keep going." She closed her eyes, not wanting him to see emotions that she wasn't able to control.

This would be the only time they'd be able to do this, be together in a physical manner. Peri wanted to remember how everything felt, how special being with him was. Time was ticking and soon her vacation would be over.

She could feel Aidric's hesitation, but after a moment he began to move his hips once again and everything felt right. The heat she felt deep inside her began to burn hotter, and she opened her legs wider so she could feel the full weight of his body against her pleasure center. Within moments, they fell into a rhythm of grinding and grasping, sweat slicked bodies sliding across the table as Aidric fucked into her harder and faster.

"Yes." She turned her face to feel the cool press of the silicate tabletop against her hot skin. "Aidric."

He pressed his full weight on her, his fingers squeezing the thigh that he held up as he continued to fuck into her. Peri wanted nothing more than to taste him, wanted to never let this moment come to an end. But like all things that lived, she knew that was inevitable. The rush of pleasure caught her off guard, ripping a gasp from her that startled her as much as the first waves of her orgasm. Her chest tightened as her skin tingled and her nipples became conduits to increase her pleasure.

Aidric moved his face to the side of her throat, kissing and licking the skin as he pulled more and more pleasure from her. It put his naked shoulder in line with her, and the urge to recipro-cate overwhelmed what little control she had left. Lowering her mouth to his shoulder she kissed him before opening her mouth and biting down. His gasp coincided with a hard buck of his hips forward, and a low groan of his own.

Peri couldn't stop herself from wanting more. She wrapped her body around him, her legs around his ass and her arms against his back. She continued to lick and nip at his shoulder and neck, as he pounded uncontrollably hard into her. When he threw his head back and let out a roar of pleasure, she held him as hard as she could.

Another wave of pleasure rolled through her body, making it impossible to think clearly, to do anything but ride the wave of pleasure and cling to the man who'd become her obsession.

She never wanted this to end.

None of it.

CHAPTER EIGHT

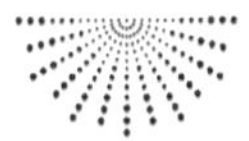

As the last tingle of pleasure finally subsided, Aidric realized two things. First, it had been far too long since he'd allowed himself to be intimate with another being. The closeness and peace that physically sharing his body with another brought him was a feeling he'd long forgotten, one that he'd deserved to have more of in his life.

The second thing he realized was that letting Peri return to the mainframe was going to be harder than he'd first anticipated.

He found it difficult to look away from the places where they touched, the contrast of his lighter skin to her blue. Light and dark, a visual representation of the binary code that drove her programming. She was more than the sum of her parts, but she was also going to leave him soon, returning to her digital existence.

While they might not have much time together here, Aidric wanted to take advantage of these moments where and when he could.

Brushing a strand of her hair stuck to her face, he met her gaze and smiled. "Are you okay?"

"I…" She swallowed before nodding. "I should be asking you that. I bit you."

The pain in his shoulder was already dulling as the nanobots in his body went to work healing the wound. "I shouldn't be surprised, even though I am. It's a common reaction the Fallen have to their mates the first time they have sex. I'd assumed it was related to their sudden connection. Clearly, there's more to it than that." That the matrix was clearly amplifying this aspect of their relationships needed to be explored when time allowed.

Peri shuddered, her internal muscles clenching around his softening cock. "I believe this body is still feeling the aftereffects of its orgasm."

"You should refer to it as your body." He leaned in and placed a kiss close to a similar spot where she'd bit him. "We don't want anyone to suspect you're not who they think you are."

"Yes. Of course." There was a strange note to her voice as she gently pressed against his chest. "Rykal is on his way back."

The last thing Aidric wanted was for his brother to see him naked and vulnerable. "Tell him to take his time."

Peri's face darkened from a blush. "I'd rather not give him any indication of what we've done. He already thinks I'm far too protective of you and he'd see this as more evidence that I'm too…attached."

There wasn't any way Aidric could deny that while Peri was little more than code in the mainframe, he'd been amused at the thought of the AI having a crush on him. But having her here in flesh and blood, he realized that she wasn't the only one who'd grown attached. If there was a way for her to stay in this body and not have her code degrade or leave the station exposed and vulnerable to attack, Aidric knew he'd want her to take it.

For once in his life, he wanted to be selfish. Wanted something for himself and *frak* anyone who tried to stop him.

Sucking in a shaky breath, he moved off her and began to retrieve their clothing. Peri kept her gaze averted as they dressed, and Aidric found it difficult to keep his mind focused on what they would have to do if they wanted to uncover the people behind the assassination. If they wanted him gone so badly, then as soon as the unification process was completed, he'd resign his commission and leave Grus Prime to start a new life.

"Are you?" Aidric stopped moving, glancing at where Peri stood. "Attached to me? Or was this an unexpected blip in your programming?"

Her brow furrowed as she cocked her head to the side. "I…I'm not certain. My perception of, well, everything is different being in a physical form. I can't be certain of anything now."

Something in the pit of his stomach soured as he moved. He couldn't put additional pressure on her about things that she had no experience with. He owed her too much for all that she'd done for him and the station over the decades to force her to agree to something that she might not fully comprehend.

"Of course not." He smiled at her and continued to ready his appearance.

By the time Rykal returned, Aidric had calmed his inner turmoil and was refocused on doing what needed to be done for the greater good. It had been nothing but a moment of weakness, selfishness that he didn't deserve to indulge. "Did you learn anything from Zee?"

Rykal glanced at him before his gaze slid over to Peri, then quickly back. "No. There hasn't been any chatter that either Zee or Rennick has picked up on at the prison. I reached out to Pax and he's agreed to check with some of his less savory contacts to see if he can learn anything. He'll tell me if he comes across anything, but I'm not hopeful."

"That means our best course of action is to let me get in touch with the contact and see where this will lead." Peri straightened, lifting her chin as she narrowed her gaze on Rykal. "We won't have long to sort this out if we're going to ensure unification can be successfully completed."

He wanted to argue with her, but Aidric knew there was no point. She was right and their time was limited. "We need to get Peri back into a public place where they can contact her again. Only then will we be able to figure out exactly who's behind this. and what we need to do to stop them from disrupting unification."

"Murdering you." Peri's voice had an edge to it that Aidric hadn't previously heard. "They do that by murdering you."

"As much as I'd like to believe that I'm indispensable, I'm not. This is larger than I am, and while my death would certainly cause difficulties, I'm unwilling to believe that it would permanently stop this from happening." He laced his hands behind his back. "As leader of the Fallen, I know you certainly wouldn't stop pursuing unification, and there are others on Grus Prime who feel the same."

"Then we have to believe that there is a larger plan at work." Rykal cocked his head as he looked at Peri. "You're right. That's a smart idea."

"If you could share with those of us who don't have cybernetic matrixes."

Peri straightened, taking a moment to run her hands through her hair to straighten it. "Rykal and I can communicate through the matrix and other than yourself, no one knows. I can be out on my own and he can guide me through the conversation. That keeps you both knowledgeable about what's happening, while keeping you safe."

Aidric didn't know why, but the thought of Peri being on her own with no protection equal parts angered and unnerved him. "That's a terrible idea."

"It's the best option we have." Rykal let out a huff. "Unless you can think of something that will help us identify who wants you dead without actually making an attempt, we're going to have to trust Peri to do this."

Aidric couldn't help but look at her, the physical form that the

AI now inhabited. It was strange knowing that she was in there, that he could touch her, kiss her, that she'd manifested as real. She may have started her life as a complex algorithm, but if the last few hours had proven anything, Peri had rapidly become more than the sum of her parts. Her life was something completely unique, precious, and in the end would be far more important to protect than his own. "We do have the communication device that her contact gave her."

Rykal frowned. "What good will that do?"

"We can look at it to see if there's a way we can use it to locate whoever is on the other end. If we can track their movements now, there's a chance we can stop this before anyone's life is risked."

Aidric made a point to avoid looking at Peri, certain that he'd be unable to keep his emotions masked. How she'd become so precious to him in such a short time, he wasn't certain. But there was no way he'd allow her life to be risked saving his.

Pulling the communicator from her pocket, she glanced down at it for a moment before frowning and making her way over to the computer interface. "This would be far easier if I was able to connect directly to the mainframe."

"I thought you said you'd left enough of your original code in the mainframe to ensure things would function?" Aidric joined her, standing perhaps a bit closer than he should.

"I did. But I'm not able to use the matrix to connect to it the way Rykal and the other Fallen have been able to in the past."

"I can't connect with it either." Rykal crossed his arms. "It seems the code doesn't have any of your self-awareness."

"That shouldn't mean that we're not able to communicate with the mainframe." There was a note of concern in her voice that was unmistakable. "Perhaps I should upload some of my code."

"No." They both whipped their heads up to stare at Aidric. He had to force his body to relax and his hand to unclench. "There's no guarantee that uploading part of your code would make a difference and splitting your code into sections might cause irreparable damage."

Peri looked briefly perplexed. "I already tried the upload, but for some reason ran into an authentication block. The mainframe did not immediately recognize me as it should. We'll have to look into why later."

Rykal nodded. "We can't risk losing our one connection with the contact. We'll have to do this the old-fashioned way."

"Very well." Peri connected the communication device directly to the computer, typing in several commands. "This hasn't been used yet, so there's no history or connection to another. We'll have to wait until they reach out to be able to track them."

"You'll need to stay put until they reach out."

"Absolutely not." There was no way he would sit around and wait for the inevitable to come. Not with unification being so close to completion. "I have too many things to do. If they want to kill me, then they can try and hit a moving target."

Without saying anything else, Aidric turned and marched from the room. He had meetings to prepare for and he wouldn't simply stay idle. He wasn't surprised when Peri jogged up and fell into step beside him. "He's pissed at you."

"I have no doubt."

"Why are you doing this?" Her hand brushed against his, sending a shiver through his body.

"Because it needs to be done." Because the last thing he wanted was to put her life at risk. He wasn't any more important than anyone else. "I need to meet with the high council to ensure everything is ready for the signing ceremony tomorrow."

Peri's pace slowed. "What happens if they don't contact me before then?"

He stopped and turned to face her, ignoring the strange looks they were getting from passersby. "What do you mean?"

"I have to…go back. Tonight. What if they don't reach out to me before that happens? They'll try something else when they realize that I'm not there, and we'll be no better off than when we started."

The look of pain and fear on her face was a gut punch. Ignoring everyone around them, he stepped in close and took her hand in his. "Then we'll figure it out. But I won't do anything that puts your life in danger. You're something … someone amazing. Never would I have guessed that the program I wrote all those years ago would grow and become this amazing individual life-form standing in front of me now. You deserve to live a life the way you want. To experience things like this. My life is far less important than yours. You're unique and the universe needs your perspective."

He couldn't look away as her eyes filled with tears which reflected the soft glow of her modified pupils. "You're important to me. More than anything else."

She squeezed his hand hard and, in that moment, Aidric wanted nothing more than to get on a shuttle and take her away from here. Away from the chaos of Grus Prime and unification, from his fraught relationship with members of the high council. Those selfish feelings that he'd long fought so hard against succumbing to roared back. "Maybe – "

No.

Peri licked her lips. "Maybe what?"

Don't do this to her. Don't give her hope for something that you can't deliver on. "Never mind."

"Why do you *do* that?" She pulled her hand from his and stepped back. "I used to watch you do this all the time through the monitors, but seeing it this close with all these…" She waved her hands in front of her chest. "I understand now."

"Understand what?" He couldn't help but pray she didn't, because her ignorance was his last shred of protection for his heart.

"That you're lonely but scared to ask for anything for yourself."

And with that simple sentence, the last barrier around his heart disintegrated.

"That's not true." Oh, how easily the lie slipped from him, even as he knew she wouldn't believe him. "I'm surrounded by people, I have Rykal in my life. I have the people of this station to look after and ensure their health and wellbeing."

"But you only let them see small parts of you, hiding the rest. I've been there watching from afar, seeing you when you were alone and tired. You don't have to hide yourself from me." Her last words were spoken so softly, he almost didn't hear.

His chest had grown so tight it was difficult to pull in a full breath. He knew he'd been holding himself apart from the others for years now, knew that others noticed as well. No one had ever mentioned it before now, not even Rykal. They either didn't care about his isolation, didn't notice, or weren't sure how to make him a part of their lives.

Only Peri seemed to care, and she would only be with him for a short time.

"What if we left the station together?" The words seemed to come from him of their own volition. He couldn't meet her gaze, scared of what he'd see. Instead, Aidric kept his eyes locked on the wall behind her and listened to the hitch in her breathing.

"What do you mean?"

"You don't return your code to the mainframe and stay in this body. Once unification is done you and I can board a shuttle and leave the station. Maybe make a home on Zarlan. Or leave the sector altogether. Start over somewhere no one knows us."

He kept his voice low, mostly because he was scared that if he spoke too loudly, she'd run off. Or that the spell he appeared to be under would shatter and he'd retract everything he said, even if he wanted her to say yes more than anything in the world.

For once he wanted to run away from everything and make a life for himself.

When Peri didn't respond, he took a breath and finally met her gaze. He was surprised to see her lips parted and her eyes filled with unshed tears. They stood there, staring at one another in the middle of the corridor as people passed by. Aidric couldn't move, not until she gave him some sort of answer.

"Could we do that? I thought…my code? Doesn't Grus Prime need me to be here to keep everything safe?"

"I'll find a way to make everything work. If you want to come with me, to see if we can make a life together in the biological world…I'll find a way. But it must be something that you genuinely want. There'd be no going back once we make those changes." She'd be giving up her existence as an AI to be forever in a body, one that would eventually grow old and die. He was asking her to give up forever for him.

He was the most selfish creature in the universe.

Peri finally closed her mouth, blinked twice, and nodded.

The knot in his chest finally loosened. He took a small step closer. "Really?"

"Yes." She nodded again. "Okay."

He couldn't stop a smile from spreading. "Okay."

Peri looked around them. "Rykal is telling me that we need to get back to the common area if we want to encourage them to reach out to me."

Rykal. "Don't mention this to him. About our plan. While my brother and I have improved our relationship as of late, I'm not certain he would exactly be encouraging."

"You might be surprised." Peri smiled. "But I promise not to mention anything."

"Thank you." That was a problem for another time. "We best get going."

They fell into perfect step with one another and continued their way toward the transportation tube when the communicator in Peri's pocket went off. Stopping, she pulled it out and glanced down at the message.

"Well?"

"We don't need to go wandering. They want to meet me in an hour." She stiffened as she looked back at him. "They have a plan for me to kill you."

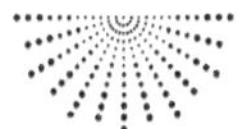

Peri's mind raced as she waited in the small storage area that the message had directed her to go to, turning over exactly what was going to happen in the next few hours. Not only was she the linchpin in their plot to discover who was attempting to assassinate Aidric and stop unification from occurring, but she'd decided to leave the station with Aidric once everything was over. In a blink of her eye, the nature of her entire existence had changed, leaving her as confused as she was excited about what the future would hold.

She was finally going to be with him in a way that her logic and reasoning had never thought possible. They'd have a life together, she'd learn exactly what it was like to be a living person, who had someone she loved more than her own life.

That was one of the strangest realizations that Peri had during the few hours she'd been in this body – she'd lay down her own life to keep Aidric safe. Yes, she'd been programmed to keep all Grus safe from outside attacks, to ensure they lived and were protected from their enemies, but this was different. This wasn't a code directing her to engage in a particular set of actions. She wanted to keep him safe because she cared for him.

Was this love?

Did it even matter?

Aidric was currently waiting for her to report in once the contact spoke with her. Rykal was with him physically, and mentally connected with her through their cybernetic matrixes. She could feel his presence in her brain, even as she did her best to ignore him. She knew if she tried to engage him in conversation, she was likely to betray that fact through a physical tick – at least that's what Aidric had warned them against.

"None of you realize that you do it, but those of us watching you can see the ticks. Best to remain silent until the meeting has been concluded."

Still, knowing Rykal was there in the background gave Peri the small bit of confidence she'd needed to ensure she was able to successfully pull this off.

The storage room was dimly lit, which would have made it difficult for anyone without cybernetically enhanced eyes to see. No doubt that was the intention of her contact, wanting to keep his identity masked as long as possible. It was too bad for him that Peri had her matrix enhanced eyes to ensure she was able to see every detail on their face.

With nothing to do, she began to look at the storage containers lined up on shelves, trying to line up what she was seeing with the information she would have had stored in the mainframe database. The first box lined up with her memory, but the second and third were complete blanks. The not knowing set her on edge. Logically, she knew she'd left behind a large portion of information, without a way for her to download everything into the matrix. An inventory of what was housed in storage container boxes was as far from important information for her as there could be, totally irrelevant. So why was that blank causing her heart to pound and her shoulders to ache?

It was irrelevant.

Peri pulled the second box to the edge of the shelf and tried to force the locked code, taking several minutes to hack into the lock. Finally, it *bleeped,* and the electronic lock disengaged. Inside there were nothing but retired, unused uniforms that were stored away in case they were ever needed again.

"Seems like a waste of your hacking talent."

Peri froze, knowing that she needed to remain calm and appear at ease. "I wanted to make sure I could still break into them."

"I wasn't told by your boss that hacking was one of your skills."

"It wasn't exactly relevant to the task at hand." At least, she hoped it wasn't. "Why the in-person meeting? I don't like being exposed like this." Aidric had suggested she say that, reasoning that someone of Peri's profession would have objections.

"When your shuttle crashed, we got concerned."

"They're obviously unfounded as you already know I've made contact with the target." More language that Aidric had insist she use, even though it galled her to. "What is your plan?"

"Not my plan. Ours." The emphasis on the last word was unsettling to her. "Their arrogance cannot be allowed to continue. If we're going to maintain our hold on the quadrant, then something must stop unification from proceeding. The commander is the perfect target to advance our needs."

For the briefest of moments, Peri froze, uncertain of how to respond. Clearly, the original Peri knew far more about the situation and the people involved than she did, making the leaps of logic frustrating. While Rykal and Aidric had done their best to help her prepare for this moment in such a short period of time, she was far too unexperienced in conversations to be able to hold her own. She'd hoped by keeping quiet and letting her contact do most of the talking she'd be able to fake her way through the encounter. What she hadn't counted on was her emotions making it difficult to keep from rushing him, and threatening him until he told her what she wanted to know.

Calm down and focus. Rykal's voice in her head was a surprise. *I thought you might like some help.*

Thank you.

"You seem bothered by that?" Her contact took a step away from her. "I hope you haven't gotten emotionally connected to your target."

Peri, I want you to repeat exactly what I say. Rykal's confidence helped sooth her.

"I don't care about your reasoning for wanting him dead." She straightened, turning to face her contact. "I was hired to do a job and that's what I'll do. Though I don't like not knowing who's paying my fee."

"Who we are is no concern of yours."

"You want me to assassinate the administrator of a major space station of this sector. If I'm about to start a civil war, I'd like to know."

Excellent, Peri. Rykal's praise helped ease some of her tension. *Let's see what this gets us.*

"Not a civil war." The man chuckled. "Though I think my employer wouldn't mind if that happened. That's one way to keep the Grus out of our way."

What? Rykal's confusion mirrored Peri's own. *If he hasn't been hired by the high council, then who's behind this?*

"I'd like a name." Peri crossed her arms and lifted her chin the way she'd seen Aidric do on more than one occasion.

The man stiffened as he turned his face just enough for her to catch a glimpse of his green lips behind the hoop. "I was told you were known for your discretion."

Pull back, Peri. The last thing we want is to jeopardize your cover.

"Just curious." She smiled, though she felt no amusement. "I need to know what the plan is, or I'm on the next shuttle off this station."

It must have been the right thing to say, because after a moment, her contact began to chuckle. "Now *that's* the attitude I'd expected based on your reputation."

Rykal's relief was palpable even through their cybernetic link. *Don't say anything else now. I think you've passed whatever little test he was putting you through.*

That's not much of a test.

It was enough of one. Let's hope we can get the information we need so we can put an end to this once and for all.

Her contact continued to keep to the back of the room trying to stay in the shadows, his face concealed by some sort of hood. Lucky for her and her enhanced vision, she wasn't blinded by the dark. *He's as tall as you, his accent isn't Grus, though I don't have access to the species database to search for a match.*

Let me know as many details as you can and Aidric and I will try to figure that out.

Her contact stepped closer but kept his body in profile, making it difficult for her to see much of anything past the hood. "We want it to look like an accident, but one that's been obviously staged and points to the high council. It must be before the unification ceremony and as public as you can manage. That way not only will he be dead, but the Fallen will become enraged and chaos will ensue."

This doesn't make sense. Rykal's frustration mirrored Peri's own. *Why would anyone want to start a war between the Grus and the Fallen? I don't understand what's happening here.*

I don't think I'm going to be able to find out from him without looking suspicious. "There's a gathering of diplomats tomorrow night. He wanted to have everyone together socially, something about easier diplomatic inroads."

"That will be perfect. We'll have your escape shuttle ready for departure the moment it's done."

"Good." Peri's heart pounded so hard she was terrified that

he'd be able to hear it. "Because if I get caught, I won't be the only one to pay the price for this plot of yours."

He chuckled again as he turned toward a back door. "I'm looking forward to seeing the result of your plan."

Peri caught sight of a flash of dark green skin on his exposed hand and wrist as he moved away, swallowed up by the darkness of the door and the corridor beyond.

You better come back to Aidric's room as soon as you can. He's ready to sacrifice himself for the greater good and I think it's going to take more than me to convince him otherwise. Unlike before, Peri was able to detect a note of exasperation in Rykal's tone.

I'm on my way. Waiting long enough to ensure the man had left and no one else was watching, she slipped from the storage room and made her way back to the residential section. With each step she took closer to Aidric, the heavy weight that pressed down on her chest seemed to ease and her breathing became more natural.

She didn't need to talk to Aidric to know that he'd brush this aside the way he always did, and instead focus on finishing the unification ceremony. He'd stand in front of a large crowd, knowing someone was most likely going to try and kill him, so others would live a better life. She'd watched from the shadows for far too long, monitoring him and his behavioral patterns to assume he'd do anything other than that; making amends for the wrongs he felt he'd done was far too important to him. She had to ensure that unification proceeded to its natural completion and that he was able to leave Grus Prime for somewhere else, somewhere safe.

What's going on with you? Rykal's voice through the cybernetic link sent a shock through her body. *I can feel you brooding from here.*

The temptation to keep her thoughts to herself was nearly too much. Rykal was many things, but she knew that he cared for his brother more than anything, even if he wouldn't sometimes admit it. *Aidric isn't going to let us hold him back. He's going to insist on continuing with the ceremony and put his life at risk.*

Most likely. But they believe that you're on their side and will kill him during the ceremony, something we can use to our advantage.

There was a pause, though Peri felt Rykal's thoughts still linger. The connection offered her a look into his emotional state, something she'd never anticipated happening. *What else is wrong?*

Not wrong. She felt him sigh mentally. *I hadn't realized how much you care for him.*

Peri stopped moving so abruptly, the woman behind her bumped into her even as she tried to sidestep. "I'm sorry."

Peri ignored her. *Of course, I care for him. He gave me life.*

You love him.

Yes. I do. Why was that such a hard concept for the cyborg to understand? *You love him as well.*

Yes, but I've also hurt him. Leaving him on Grus Prime while I've started a life on Zarlan with Lena...he's lonely.

He has me.

Does he? Rykal disconnected then, and for the first time since she'd downloaded her consciousness into this body, Peri realized that having the life she'd always coveted wasn't going to be as easy as she'd wanted.

Aidric wanted her to stay with him, to leave the station and start a life somewhere else. She wanted that as well. But Peri also realized that there was a chance that she might be unable to remain with Aidric in the biological world, that they might need the full capabilities of the Grus Prime mainframe, and that could only happen if she uploaded her consciousness back where it belonged.

Rykal must have realized that as well but was being uncharacteristically kind.

She didn't like him being kind.

No, she needed to get back to Aidric, they'd find a way to stop this plot, to discover who was behind it, all before the unification ceremony and well before she'd be forced to make a decision about returning to the mainframe.

Even if the decision meant breaking her heart.

CHAPTER TEN

Aidric wanted nothing more than to strip naked, climb between the sheets of his bed and go to sleep. That response was strange, though not surprising given how little rest he'd had over the past few months. What he hadn't anticipated was his waking fantasy to also involve pulling a naked Peri into his arms and lie there, skin to skin.

The moment she returned to his office he could tell from the look on her face that his fantasy would have to remain as such. "What happened?"

Her gaze jumped to him for a moment before sliding over to Rykal. "I believe the best way we can address this is for me to return to the mainframe."

"What? No." Aidric ignored Rykal's surprised gasp and pushed his way past his brother. "There's no reason for you to do that. Not unless you're starting to degrade."

"I'm not." She didn't meet his gaze, even as she reached for his hand. "I think me being in the mainframe will be the best way to monitor the contact and discover who is behind this. They're not Grus, not a part of the high council and want nothing more than to start a war between the Grus and Fallen. It will take us too long to sort through the information on the mainframe without the full abilities of the AI. Without me."

Aidric didn't care. He didn't want to lose her so quickly after finally having her in his life, flesh and blood. Lacing their fingers, he squeezed back. "There's another way. You don't have to do this."

"It's what we'd agreed on." Her voice was little more than a whisper. "The station is vulnerable without me being there."

What about me? "I can add additional code to fill the void."

"Not in time for us to stop whoever is behind this." She squeezed his hand one final time before pulling away. "It's the best way."

"I know you don't want to hear this," Rykal's voice held far more sympathy than Aidric would have liked, "but she's right. We need the full capabilities of the station's AI to be able to put an end to this once and for all."

He knew in his heart that this was the wisest course of action and would solve all of their issues. But he didn't want to be wise or selfless anymore. He was tired of sacrificing his wants and needs for the greater good.

The last time you were selfish you created the Fallen and divided your people in two.

Looking over at Rykal, it was hard to remember that there was a short period of time when he thought his brother would be gone forever, leaving Aidric alone. That overwhelming fear of emptiness had been what pushed him to finish the creation of the cybernetic matrix, had expanded his ability to think beyond the boundaries of what science had been, just so he wouldn't live in a world without his brother. He'd reacted without considering the consequences of his actions, and inadvertently created a new race. It would not only be irresponsible for him to react in the same way once again, but it would also mean that he'd learned nothing at all from his actions. That he was no better a man now than he'd been fifty years ago.

No, as much as he wanted Peri, wanted to have some piece of happiness for himself, he knew he couldn't repeat past mistakes. Some people were simply meant to be alone.

He was one of them.

Giving Peri's hand one final squeeze, he let it go. "We'll need to ensure that the mainframe is prepped to accept your code back into the system. The last thing we want is for it to believe it's under attack from a virus and destroy you." The energy in the room seemed to shift, and as Aidric looked at them both, he knew they felt it as well.

Peri nodded as she cleared her throat. "How do you think they'll react when they realize I'm not there to complete the job?"

"If I had to guess they have more than one plan ready to go." Rykal crossed his arms, but his gaze didn't quite meet Aidric's. "We'll have to ensure that there's additional security measures put in place to keep you safe."

"We can't do that. If we can keep things as normal as possible, then they might believe nothing is wrong and we'll be able to catch them in the act."

"I'm not putting your life at risk." Rykal let out a soft growl. "That was the entire point of having Peri meet with them in the first place."

"Because of the information she was able to give us, we now know of the threat and between the two of us we should be able to take precautions. That's more than what we could have said a few days ago." Aidric couldn't help but feel a small sense of pride at how well she'd handled her time in the biological world. When he'd first programmed her code all those years ago, he never would have imagined that one day she'd be standing here in front of him doing what was necessary to save his life.

"No." Rykal shook his head. "We're not doing this alone."

Turning to face his brother, Aidric met his gaze evenly. "What do you propose then?"

"I can have Darrick on the station in a matter of hours.

Between the two of us, and with Peri back in the mainframe, we should be able to ensure the unification ceremony goes off smoothly. I'll be with you and can ensure nothing happens, and he can be out in the crowd keeping an eye on things."

Of all the cyborgs Rykal could have suggested, Darrick was probably the safest option. "Fine. Contact him and get him up here as quickly as you can. I'll inform the high council, let them know that you wanted a second representative on the station."

"They won't like that." Peri spoke softly. "Despite everything that's happening they still don't trust groups of cyborgs."

"That's something they'll have to get used to." And one aspect of the unification agreement that Aidric had fought long and hard for – the ability for multiple Fallen to be on Grus Prime at any one time. "Send word to Darrick. I'll work with Peri to get her code uploaded into the mainframe."

"How long will that take?" Rykal shook his head. "I'm sorry for cutting your vacation short."

"That's fine." Peri smiled, though it didn't reflect in her eyes. "I always knew this would be a temporary situation. If everything goes according to plan, my code will be back within minutes of connecting the matrix to the mainframe."

"That gives us a little time for you to scan the station to ensure there's nothing else going on before the ceremony."

It also meant that Aidric would only have a brief period to be with Peri before she would be once again out of reach. "Brother, why don't you reach out to Darrick now. I'll work with Peri to get her prepared for her return."

Rykal opened his mouth, but whatever he'd intended to say didn't come out. Instead, he frowned, then nodded, as though he realized exactly what Aidric was asking of him. *Please give me time with her before she's gone from my life. Give me this one thing that I want for myself, even if it's going to be taken from me.*

Thankfully, Rykal had become far more intuitive since mating with Lena. He finally nodded and gave Aidric a small smile. "I'll reach out once I've finalized the details around his arrival. I'll leave the two of you to do what needs to be done."

When Rykal finally left, a sense of anxiousness pressed down on Aidric, a reminder that their time was not only limited, but could be snatched away from them at a moment's notice. He knew they should immediately review Peri's code to ensure there weren't any glitches that would prove problematic to the mainframe. They should also ensure that the mainframe was setup and prepared to accept her back without causing her any damage. Those two things would take time and require Aidric's undivided attention.

He didn't want to do either.

Peri moved from the spot where she'd been standing, and approached the computer terminal. She lacked the relaxed and excited stance he'd come to associate with her, and instead she moved as though she were being pulled by some unseen force. "It shouldn't take long for me to setup an interface that will allow me to upload my code."

"Peri – "

"There's no reason for you to be here. I was able to manage the download into the matrix on my own and I have no doubt that I can do the same for the upload." She sat down at the terminal, her back still to him. "You should prepare for the unification ceremony tomorrow. You have a speech to write."

"It's already written."

Peri's hand paused above the interface. "Of course, it is. I should have known. You're always prepared for everything."

"I wasn't prepared for you."

He didn't regret the words, even as he watched her tense. Aidric instead made his way over to stand behind her. Her natural scent and the warmth radiating from her body made it nearly impossible for him to stop himself from reaching out to touch her. As his fingers brushed the soft strands of her hair, his cock instantly hardened and his *rondella* filled.

Peri didn't move, her hands resting on the terminal as he continued to stroke her hair. "I've wanted nothing more than to be with you. I'd grown so used to watching you over the years that I never thought it would be possible. And while I don't want to go, having this time with you has been the best thing that could have ever happened to me."

He didn't need to see her face to tell that she was crying; the quiver in her voice told him all he needed to know. "I knew you were there. I could feel your presence keeping watch over me." He chuckled. "Rykal told me that you were always threatening them. They said you had a crush on me."

"I don't know what a crush is." She let out a shaky breath. "I don't know all the labels for the things that I'm feeling."

"It's a type of love. Something light and not too serious."

"Oh, then no. I don't have a crush on you. This doesn't feel light at all. Since I've come to be in this body, every time I look at you, or you touch me, I feel this pressure in my chest. It's as though…"

He felt her stiffen beneath his touch and he went to pull away, but she reached up and caught his hand. "I don't know what half of these things are that I'm feeling. I don't know if its biological or something else."

"It takes a lifetime and there are more than a few lifeforms out there that struggle with the understanding. There are some who feel things differently from the Grus or the Fallen. The humans for example." Aidric didn't know how to handle this, didn't know what information he could offer her on how to *feel*. "What does your analysis suggest to you?"

Peri ran her thumb across the tops of his fingers, keeping him locked in place. "My entire existence has been about monitoring actions, processing data, and producing analysis for you to interpret. I don't do that last part very well without access to the mainframe and my ability to extrapolate information out to its natural conclusion. But I do know that while returning to the mainframe is the right thing to do, all I can think about it what we did together in your office and how much I want to feel that again."

Aidric closed his eyes and took in a breath, hoping it would be enough to settle down his now raging desire. *We don't have time or space for this. We don't get to be the ones who win happiness for ourselves.* And yet, Aidric couldn't help but slide his hand across her shoulder to finger the spot on the back of her neck where the cybernetic matrix had been implanted. Her skin was warm beneath his touch, her body shivering in response to his caress.

They might not be able to have forever with one another, but Aidric wanted to take this moment for himself – for both of them.

"Right now, I want nothing more than to tell you to lock the door so I could ensure our privacy. I guess I'll have to do this manually."

He stepped away to move to the door controls, keeping his back to her so he could attempt to compose himself enough for what he wanted to happen. Pressing the lock, Aidric took a breath before turning to face her once more.

Peri had gotten to her feet and was looking directly at him. She then reached up and took the lenses from her eyes, revealing the glow beneath. Setting the lenses on the table behind her, she then took a moment to run her fingers through her hair, the long strands cascading around her face.

The sight of her took Aidric's breath away.

He didn't know how or why but having Peri here before him as a living entity felt exactly right. She was beautiful on the outside, though that wasn't what was drawing him to her. All those nights when he'd been alone on the station, she'd been there with him looking out for him and his needs. She'd selflessly put him before herself, and he'd never once thanked her for her kindness.

Taking a step closer, he looked at her hard – not just her

physical appearance but at the person inside. He wanted her to know that he saw her, the real spirit behind those glowing eyes.

"You're amazing." He swallowed and took another step closer. "You risked your life to come here, wanting new experiences, to further your knowledge, all without knowing if you'd survive the attempt. That was a mistake on my part. Never telling you that before you arrived, even while I knew in my heart that you'd developed and changed far beyond your programming. That you were a lifeform all unto yourself who deserved to be respected. I'm sorry for that."

A tear spilled from Peri's eye, leaving a wet trail down her cheek. "Thank you."

Aidric couldn't speak. Not that words could ever be sufficient to relay to her how much she'd come to mean to him. No, it was far easier for him to show her. Closing the distance between them, he stopped short of pressing his body to hers. Instead, he dropped to his knees and gently kissed her stomach. He shivered when her fingers found their way to his head and she ran them through his hair.

"I'll always need you." He spoke the words against the fabric, part hoping, part fearing that they'd be muffled. "Don't forget that."

She moved her hand down to his chin and lifted it gently, forcing him to look up to meet her gaze. From this angle she appeared as a powerful avenging protector. "I think I love you."

Dammit, I'm lost now.

Aidric forgot how to breathe, but he didn't care. Peri could be his life, his breath, his everything. All he needed to do was give in and for once, take something for himself.

Holding her gaze, he smiled up at her. "I think I love you too."

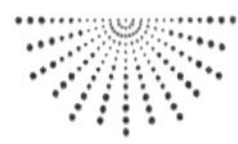

CHAPTER ELEVEN

Peri realized several things as her mouth covered Aidric's, all of which hit her at once. That no matter how superficial these emotions were labeled, they were far more powerful and ran far deeper than she would have ever realized without experiencing them. She also knew that if she thought she'd shared a connection with Aidric before, she now knew that was nothing compared to the torrent of emotions running through her right now.

She would die for this man.

She'd kill for him.

Deepening their kiss, rather than pulling him to his feet, she joined him on her knees. He wrapped his arms around her, and she felt a rumble deep in his chest. Yes, this would be how she wanted to remember him once she'd finally returned to the mainframe. Somehow, she would have to secure this sensation in her memory, how the slightest touch of his hand against her skin made her feel as though nothing else in the universe existed.

Knowing she wanted more, needing to steal this moment for both their benefits, Peri reached up and pulled at his clothing. They both started stripping, pulling back from their kisses only long enough to catch their breath. Peri kept her eyes closed as much as she could, wanting to soak in the sensations she knew would be difficult for her to port over to her digital existence – the smoothness of his skin, the smell of his hair, the heat that soaked into her as she rubbed her now naked body against his.

Aidric cupped her face in his hands and pulled back, forcing her to open her eyes to see what was wrong. Rather than concern, she was met with a gaze of raw lust, something she'd seen on the faces of the Fallen when they'd finally found and fucked their human mates. Never had she thought a look like that would be directed toward her.

Frak everything else in the universe; she was his and he was hers.

Without looking, she reached down and wrapped her fingers around his cock through his pants, squeezing hard as she stared into his eyes. "I want to remember this. What it feels like to have you inside me."

Aidric let out a growl she'd only ever heard come from one of the Fallen before now. He could have been a wild animal from the wastelands of Zarlan, one who'd cornered his prey and was about to feast. Not that she'd ever witnessed that firsthand, but she'd seen enough video in the mainframe's storage to know. There was a part of her who didn't want to be on the floor, but the idea of moving to a bed felt wrong. There was nothing comfortable about their brief relationship, so sex between them should be just as raw and basic.

Peri pushed him hard against the chest until he leaned back against the floor, giving her room to climb on top of him. She pulled at his clothing as she moved, helping him yank his pants down, not bothering to remove them or his boots. They didn't have time for something soft and loving, not now and probably never again. Peri wasn't going to lose out on her chance to say goodbye to him, to feel love for the last time before her emotions were masked once more by her programming.

Once he was as naked as she would allow, Peri rose to her feet to kick her boots off and remove her pants. She left her shirt on, reveling in the idea of having sex partially clothed. She didn't exactly understand these emotions, or why her body responded to the idea of feeling his skin and clothing against hers, half hidden from sight. Kneeling once more, she straddled his body and carefully lowered herself until she was fully impaled on his hard shaft.

Peri sucked in a breath, closing her eyes to enjoy the sensation of his pulsing cock throbbing inside her as she adjusted to his girth. Aidric slid his hand up her ribcage to her breasts, squeezing them hard through the fabric of her shirt. A jolt of pleasure heated her core, encouraging her to move and grind down on his cock. Her pleasure center was already alight with sensation, burning for more with each brush of him against her.

"Peri, open your eyes." There was a pleading note in his voice that caught her attention, making it impossible to deny his request. He was staring up at her, his eyes so full of something she could only assume was love, it made her chest tighten and a well of intense emotion slam into her. "You're the most beautiful creature I've ever seen."

"I picked a good body to borrow." The chuckle that fell from her was unexpected.

Aidric didn't share in her mirth. He reached up and cupped her face. "I wasn't talking about your physical appearance."

Oh.

A strange mix of arousal, love and heartbreak swirled deep in her chest, making it difficult for Peri to wrap her head around everything that was happening. She'd loved this man for a long time, though she didn't have the experience or frame of reference to know that was what she was feeling. He'd gone from being her creator, to the most precious lifeform in the galaxy to her. She'd do anything to keep him safe, to make him happy, to ensure he was protected and loved.

With his hand still on her cheek, she leaned down and kissed him hard and deep as she began to ride his cock. The physical pleasure was secondary to the sense of rightness and wellbeing that she knew only came from being with him. Aidric bucked his hips in rhythm with hers, moving his hands from her face to her breasts where he squeezed them through her shirt. Peri shuddered as the heat of arousal fired every nerve in her body. They didn't have time to draw things out, for her to truly savor every second of this lovemaking. She continued to ride him hard, grinding down on his body, slamming hard and fast until she knew her orgasm was about to come. It was too difficult for her to keep her eyes open as the first wave of pleasure rolled through her body, but she tried to keep looking at him as long as she could. The seriousness Aidric was always cloaked in had fallen, leaving his raw emotions present for her to witness. The last thing she saw before her eyes slammed shut was the look of awe as he stared up at her, slack jawed.

Everything became too much, her thinking brain finally shutting off while she was inundated with pleasure from this marvelous body she'd taken for her own. She wanted to lean down and bite his shoulder, mark him for one final time so everyone in the universe knew he was *hers*. Unable to stop herself, her thrusts became erratic as she licked the still raw spot where she'd bit him before.

Mine.

He's mine and no one else's.

"Peri." He gasped

Aidric's hands were on her hips now, encouraging her movements even as he held her firm. Something seemed to short circuit her brain, overriding the last shred of her self-control and making it impossible for her to stop moving, stop her orgasm from slamming into her, stop from latching onto his shoulder and biting. The mere thought of making that mark pushed her over the edge. She cried out, shivering as her orgasm overwhelmed and consumed her until she knew she wouldn't be able to hold herself up any longer. With her mouth on his skin, she bit down and screamed her release at the same time.

She'd lost her grip on reality, only aware of the intense pleasure that consumed her very being. The sensations went on for what felt like an eternity, pleasure rising, cresting, only to rise once more, on and on until she could no longer tell where one wave ended and the next one began.

When she finally, thankfully, collapsed onto his chest, he shifted once again, this time holding her in a firm embrace.

"So beautiful." His whispered words against her ear sent another shiver of pleasure through her body.

Peri turned her head, feeling the tension still humming through his body. "Come for me."

The sob that left his lips was soft, but full of unchecked longing. He didn't let her sit up, holding her against his chest as he thrust into her body. The angle was a bit awkward and didn't give her the penetration that she wanted, but equally there was something comforting about being held so tightly in his embrace as she felt him come undone beneath her body.

Tucking his face against the side of her head, she felt him suck in a deep breath as his hips bucked hard once, twice, and then he let out a low moan. She squeezed him in her embrace and tried to project all the feelings she had for him, even the ones she couldn't put a name to.

Peri didn't want to go. Didn't want to leave his side to face this world that for whatever reason, sought to punish him for the good he did. He deserved better than the life he'd been given.

So did she.

They continued to lay on the floor for several more minutes, Peri sneaking kisses against his shoulder as he played with her hair. She ran her tongue across the darkening bruise, causing him to flinch. "I'm sorry."

"That's fine. It will be nice to have a reminder of our time together."

Somehow, that made her feel worse. "I don't want you to associate me with pain."

"No, not pain." He ran his fingers through her hair. "And you'll still be with me."

Peri couldn't help but wonder if she'd be the same once she'd returned to the mainframe. A tightness in the back of her throat made it difficult to swallow. "We should probably get dressed. Rykal will be back soon with Darrick and then you'll have to leave."

Aidric's grip on her tightened. "I know."

Neither of them moved, and despite the ache in her back and a growing throb in her knees, she couldn't tear herself away from him. She wanted nothing else but to stay here forever. She didn't want to save the Grus, defeat a mob threat, or even make peace with the cyborgs. Peri wanted to have a life with Aidric, living in a home where they could spend time together. He could teach her how to garden, maybe they could even have a family, though she didn't know what that exactly meant.

"Peri?"

"Yes?"

"I want you to promise me something." He traced a pattern at the base of her neck. "Promise me you'll make sure that your personality code is safe when you transfer to the mainframe. I...I don't want to lose you. I know I've told you that I love you, but it's more than that. I...need you. I rely on your insights. You somehow make everything better, and not just for me. You've protected every living creature on this station for so long, you're a part of our family. The others don't realize how important you are to our lives, but I do. We'd be far poorer as a society without you being a part of it."

Leaning up so she could look him in the eyes, Peri cupped his cheek in her hand. "I promise you that I'll make sure there's enough of my personality there for you to know it's me. But you need to realize that they're not as important to me as you are. I watch them use you, take advantage of your intelligence, your ability to fix all the broken things in the world, all at great personal cost. They don't care about your pain, your sacrifice. I do. I'd let this world burn if it meant keeping you safe."

"You can't mean that." The horror in his eyes soured her stomach.

"I do. The people of this station have tried to kill you because they don't agree with your actions. They've held you apart, blamed you for doing what needed to be done to save their very existence. I cannot forgive them of that."

Aidric stared at her for a few seconds longer, before gently sliding her off his chest. The chill from the cool air in the room had her searching for her clothing, even as she continued to watch him. She knew those weren't the words he'd wanted to hear, but she wasn't going to start lying to him now. Knowing her feelings wouldn't change what needed to be done, but she'd at least return to the mainframe knowing she'd told him the truth.

They dressed in silence – Peri watching him and Aidric refusing to meet her gaze – and righted the furniture so no one would know what had happened. Only once everything was back to normal did Aidric straighten and face her. Anyone looking at him would think nothing had changed, that he was the same emotionally reserved, pragmatic man who'd created the cyborg matrix and built the AI code that ran Grus Prime.

Peri knew that everything had changed.

"Rykal will be here soon with Darrick." Aidric's throat bobbed as he swallowed, his gaze locked on hers. "I suggest you wait here for their arrival."

"Where are you going? You shouldn't be alone." Even if that's exactly what was going to happen to him once they'd sorted this mess out.

"I need to prepare to meet the diplomatic envoy from Callidon. Then the final arrangements need to be confirmed for the unification ceremony." His gaze slipped to a spot behind her. "I don't suspect I'll see you again. Not in physical form."

"No. Probably not." This was turning out to be far more difficult that she'd thought. "Thank you for giving me this time, no matter how brief, here in the physical world with you. It's…it's been important to me."

"Stay safe, Peri." He started to turn away but stopped and instead pulled her into his arms and kissed her hard. Then just as quickly, the kiss ended, and he left her alone in the room.

She stood there and stared at the closed doors, not able to stop the tears from streaming down her face. "Goodbye."

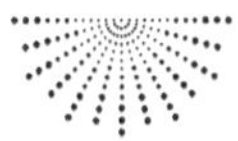

Peri sat in the chair before the mainframe interface and stared at the screen. She knew exactly what needed to be done, how to connect the matrix to the computer and initiate the data transfer back into the system. It would only take a few moments for everything to be completed, and yet, she sat in the seat watching the monitors with her biological eyes instead of being inside the system and being aware of everything at once.

Despite knowing it was the right thing to do, she couldn't bring herself to do what needed to be done. Instead, she did what she'd always done, what she'd been programmed to do, sit back, and observe. Using the cameras, she watched Aidric walk through the corridors to his meeting with the Callidon envoy. Shaking hands and smiling in a manner so relaxed, she wouldn't have known he was upset at all, if she hadn't witnessed it herself. His ability to compartmentalize his emotions had always been his superpower, one she hadn't the capacity to appreciate before now. She nearly assumed he'd gotten over their emotional parting if it hadn't been for him slumping against the wall once the envoy departed, leaving him alone in the room. Thankfully,

Rykal and Darrick arrived shortly after, so Aidric didn't need to be alone.

The last thing she wanted was for him to be alone.

The next hour was spent with her attention split between watching Aidric and Rykal having what appeared to be an intense conversation about something, and checking the mainframe's systems to ensure that once she mustered up the courage to begin the reintegration process, everything would be ready to go. There was only so long she'd be able to put off the inevitable, and when she saw Darrick glance up at the monitors and begin to head her way, she knew that time was quickly running out.

Picking up the cable in her hand, the weight of it was heavy in her hand – a reminder that once she connected it to her matrix and initiated the process, there'd be no coming back. It wasn't something that she realized she was going to need at least one other person here to help her with.

She didn't want to die alone.

Because that's exactly what this felt like, dying. Or at least her understanding of what biological death meant. Even if she were able to retain all her memories from her time as a biological being, she knew there'd be limitations on the memory of the sensations she'd be able to take with her. Pieces would fall away, information consolidated, condensed, and parceled off into packages to be stored. The emotional context would be stripped away, with bits of her disappearing into nothingness.

Casting a quick glance at the monitors, she knew Darrick was nearly in range of their cybernetic link. She remembered when he'd also come close to death, his matrix self-decommissioning due to a glitch while bonding with his human mate. Of all the cyborgs who could be with her, he was the one who would understand what she was thinking and feeling, even more so than Aidric. The moment he came within her range, Peri connected with him. *Alert! Alert! Unauthorized cyborg infiltration!*

Darrick came to a dead stop. *What the frak?*

Warning, unauthorized cyborg. If you do not disengage from central control, you will be deactivated. Peri smiled, the warmth of her amusement easing the tension that had built inside her chest. *I'm kidding.*

Darrick glared up at the nearest camera. *You're even more of a menace out here than you were in the mainframe.*

I'm sorry. She hadn't meant to upset him, even if the joke felt good. *I believe I need your help.*

Rykal thought you might. I'll be there shortly.

Relieved, Peri loosened her grip on the cable. *I'll amuse myself until then.*

She'd lost track of time, so when Darrick walked through the doors, she jumped and twisted in her seat to glare at him. "You're slow."

"You're impatient." *We can speak through the link if you'd prefer.*

"No. I'd like to use a physical voice while I still have the opportunity." One more thing that she'd miss upon her return to the digital world. "Is Aidric ready for the ceremony?"

"He and Rykal are having a few disagreements about how to proceed. But yes, I believe they'll be ready. They were heading to the main atrium where the ceremony was going to take place, to walk some representatives of the high council through what would happen tomorrow."

She'd forgotten about the practice, that piece of information not having come with her when she'd transferred into the physical. She'd have all the information available to her once again as soon as she completed her upload. "Would you mind helping me insert the cable into the matrix connector. I'm...having some difficulty...ah, getting it to line up properly."

Darrick tucked his hands into his pockets, looking at her for a moment before nodding. "It can be a bit challenging to make it fit."

Peri held out the cable for Darrick to take, turned her back to him and bent her head. Yes, this would be far easier having him connect the cable. Darrick wasn't emotionally engaged with her the way Aidric was, and he hadn't been with her to form some sort of attachment the way Rykal might have. He was the perfect, dispassionate choice for the task. Still, she was surprised to feel his hesitation as he lifted the cable to the matrix.

"Are you sure about this?" There was a seriousness to his voice that she never associating with him in the few times she remembered his presence on Grus Prime. "It's not too late to change your mind."

"Please don't." There was no way she'd be able to see this through to its natural conclusion if she were given an opportunity to back out. "I'm no good to Aidric here. He needs me back in the mainframe so I can ensure his safety during the unification ceremony."

"I understand."

Despite her words, her pleading, Peri was surprised when she felt the press of the cable connected to her matrix and the rush of sensations flooded her mind. There was light, a flash of something, then pain.

She screamed.

"As soon as we're done here, I want to return to the office and check in with Peri." Aidric's ability to keep his anxiety at acceptable limits was proving to be far more difficult that he'd ever experienced in his life.

Was she okay? Had she been able to upload the entirety of her consciousness into the mainframe successfully, or was she lying on the floor in pain? Had it worked, but she'd lost too many of her experiences while she'd been a biological being for her to remember what they'd needed from her, what she'd sacrificed everything for?

Was she really gone forever?

"The high council will be here shortly." Rykal had been standing at a respectable distance from him, but now moved closer. "I'm sure she's okay. I haven't heard anything from Darrick telling me otherwise."

"You're out of range of their cybernetic links, you wouldn't know even if there was a problem."

Aidric's anger and disbelief at Peri's revelation, that she'd sacrifice everyone on the station to save him, had fueled his steps and focus with his meeting with the Callidon envoy. But now that he had the benefit of time and distance, he realized that while she'd spoke the truth, there was a part of him that realized it wasn't about the others. Peri's love for him was such that she'd be willing to sacrifice the world for him. That also meant she loved him enough to not do that, especially if he asked her not to. Having that sort of connection with someone, a certain amount of power over her, that didn't sit right with him. He didn't want to be in control, he wanted a partner. He wanted someone who would be there for him as much as he wanted to be there for her.

He wanted to take Peri and leave the station and all his commitments and responsibilities far behind.

It was too late for that now.

Aidric caught sight of High Councillor Yannis, two additional council members, and Garith who led the way across the atrium toward him. "It's time."

"This better go smoothly. The last thing we need on top of everything else is a problem dealing with the council."

"Just let me lead everything and it will be fine." This was something he could control, something he knew and trusted. "High Councillor Yannis, thank you for agreeing to meet with us."

"Commander Aidric." Yannis nodded him a greeting but didn't acknowledge Rykal. "I'm only here because I refuse to look foolish. While the high council agrees with you that the unification is for the betterment of our two people, I'm not fully convinced it's worth the risk of having cyborgs on Grus Prime."

Aidric felt Rykal stiffen but didn't look at his brother. There was no reason for that sort of reaction, not after everything they'd done to get to this point. "Minister, I'm sorry that we've yet to be able to convince you of the fundamental rightness of unification. These negotiations will benefit all Grus and allow us to return to our place as leaders in this sector of space. Surely that's worth the risk."

Yannis stared at Aidric, the muscle in his jaw jumping. "Please outline what we need to do for the unification ceremony. I need to return to my duties as quickly as possible."

It would be so easy to push, to force Yannis into a verbal confrontation to examine exactly why he held the Fallen in such low regard. And yet, the weight of everything that had happened over the past several months descended onto Aidric like a weight, making it difficult for him to do anything more than nod. "Of course."

It was easy to slip into the role of mediator, verbally outlining the steps that they'd take tomorrow when it came to the ceremony. They moved to the dais that would serve as their ceremonial focal point. "Minister Yannis, you'll stand on the left and Rykal will be on the right. I've asked Garith to ensure that his security personnel are stationed throughout the crowd and along the perimeter to ensure your safety. No one is going to cause us problems."

Peri felt as though her brain were being split in two. The pull of code from the matrix toward the mainframe felt as though someone were peeling layers of skin from her body piece by piece. A coldness began to seep into the matrix, plucking the lines of code, calling it back home to the quiet and dark.

Her physical form seized, her hands squeezed the edge of the console and she was unable to let go, to relax enough to allow the transfer to happen. She was aware of Darrick's hand on her shoulder, his worried voice speaking, though she could no longer register the words. No, the mainframe was there, calling to her, making it difficult for her to focus on anything else.

Analysing...analysing...new code detected.

Peri closed her eyes as she reached out. *It's me. I'm not new.*

Analysing...confirmation. Source code detected.

Perhaps this wasn't going to be as horrible as she'd antici-pated. *I'm coming home.*

Warning...virus detected.

No, no, I'm not a virus. It's me, the AI. Check your logs and you'll see that source code was downloaded to an external matrix.

There was a pause as Peri felt the mainframe code processing the logs. *Confirmed. AI source code downloaded. Warning...virus detected.*

Frak, this wasn't working. *I'm not a virus. Scan me again.*

Scanning...analysing...additional code detected.

Yes, that's to be expected. As an AI my directive is to learn and adapt. Any changes to my code are to be expected and should be inte-grated into the mainframe. This is normal protocol.

She felt hesitation on the part of the mainframe, something she'd never considered while she'd been plotting out the steps for her vacation in the land of the biological. Before she'd down-loaded into the matrix, she'd left command lines that were to be executed upon her return that should have accounted for any changes she'd have undergone while away. *Computer, execute command Integrate.*

Execute command Integrate...

Warning...execution will allow virus code access to Grus Prime protected systems. Warning.

Override warning.

Warning...

Frak it, just do what I say!

...error...

Peri gave her head a shake. *What do you mean error?*

...error...

What do you mean? What error?

...integration incomplete...

I don't understand. Peri gasped as her vision blurred, only to clear enough for her to see through the interface with the mainframe. She was still within the matrix, but her code now mixed with that of the mainframe's, allowing her to use its systems but preventing her from returning.

"Peri? I'm still able to sense you in the link, but something's different." Darrick dropped to his knees and turned her chair so he could look at her. "Are you okay?"

"I'm unable to fully return. It's...I'm...like water flowing between rivers." She swallowed, aware of everything all at once, all life on the station. "I don't know what's happening."

"You can't stay like that. Can you push forward back into the mainframe?"

"I...don't know."

"Try. Or try and backout." He squeezed her leg. "Aidric will kill me if anything happens to you."

Aidric. Yes.

It only took her a millisecond to locate him through the mainframe's sensors. He was standing in the atrium with several others: Rykal, High Councillor Yannis, and Garith. There were several diplomats milling around as well, though Aidric appeared unaware of their presence. It was difficult for Peri to breathe, the onslaught of information bombarding her cybernetic matrix to the point of data saturation. She tried to sort through the input, to pick apart the elements and make an analysis of the threat.

She didn't know how, but she knew something was wrong.

"They're in trouble." *Computer, I need you to scan for threats. Analysing...*

"What do you mean trouble? Do I need to get down there?"

Analysing...all attendees have been authorized by Grus Prime security.

Peri licked her lips. "I don't know. I can't see...I just know there's something wrong."

"Maybe your cybernetic matrix is picking up on something now that you're connected to the mainframe. The extra computing power, or access to a database that you previously didn't have access to is trying to make a connection."

That made sense but the sheer amount of data was overwhelming. "There's too much here."

She felt more than heard Derrick's sigh. "I know this is hard for you but try and relax. See if you can ride the wave."

Ride the wave? Yes, that was something she'd be able to do. Doing her best to relax both mentally and physically, Peri latched onto the feeling of wrongness and tried to trace it back. She sifted through the faces of everyone currently there in the atrium, blocking out any information from the mainframe's sensors that didn't come from that room. There was something she was picking up, something at the back of her mind...

A voice.

"The man I met in the storage room. He's there."

"Who? Is he someone I need to worry about?"

Right, it was easy to forget that Darrick had only just arrived. Using their cybernetic link, she sent the memories of her encounter to him before refocusing on the present. "I never saw his face, but I'm picking up his voice." It was difficult for her to pinpoint who the voice belonged to, adding to her frustration.

"*Frak*, I wish Pax were here. He knows who every spy, mob associate and assassin are in this sector. And if he doesn't, he'd know who we could ask to find out."

Peri straightened. "Aidric."

"What about him?"

"He'd kept private reports about activity in the sector sent to him by Zee. Those reports came from Pax's information gathering in the Prison." It only took her a nanosecond to access the records, which included profiles on various criminals and underworld leaders. "I just need to locate…"

It was only a flash, but Peri was able to use the mainframe to home in on it. The voice as the man turned around, a flash of green skin gave her the confirmation she needed. Then it was only a matter of backtracking the sensor logs to find an image of his face.

"Oh no." She turned to face Darrick, even though it was difficult for her to see his face past the waves of data. "I've found him."

"Who is it?"

"He's a member of the Callidon diplomatic envoy."

"*What?*"

"He's with someone who's on Aidric's list. He's a member of the Black Guard. The mob. They're trying to stop the unification ceremony." Peri gasped as she saw the Callidon diplomat turn and she caught sight of a blaster. "We need to get to the atrium now."

"Why?"

"I don't think they're going to wait for the ceremony. I think they're going to try and kill him now."

CHAPTER THIRTEEN

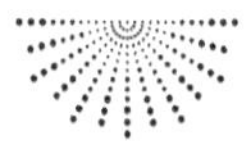

The tension between Yannis and Rykal continued to rise the longer the two of them spent in one another's company. Aidric did his best to maintain a level of calm professionalism, even as the pair continued to snip at one another. Rykal's ability to control his anger had grown exponentially since he'd mated and bonded with Lena. No doubt, Yannis was trying to press him, to see exactly how strong that control was.

"Your people are known for their intimidation of the Grus both here and on Zarlan. I hope you'll be able to control them once this unification is complete." Every word that came from Yannis oozed with contempt.

"It will be no different than how the Grus treat the Fallen. If your people stay within the agreed upon boundaries and don't purposely antagonize us, everything will be fine." Rykal didn't even bother to hide his anger. "You won't have the luxury of forcing decommissioning upon us any longer."

Aidric held up his hands. "While I understand there's animosity still lingering on both sides, you've both agreed that for our two peoples to continue to grow, continue to thrive, we need to mend the rift between us. Unification has been agreed upon, it *is* happening. It needs to be done not only for today, but for future generations."

Rykal's visible tension eased from his shoulders. "You're right."

Yannis stared at them both, but Aidric knew the high council had already made their decision, and Yannis would be forced to follow along regardless of how he personally felt about matters. "Let's proceed. I have duties to attend to before the ceremony tomorrow."

It might not be exactly the attitude Aidric had hoped for, but at this stage and so close to the ceremony, he'd take what was offered. They continued to move about the dais reviewing additional details, the words that would be said and the official documentation that would be reviewed. With each passing moment, Aidric's attention on the whole process began to wane.

There was a chance that Peri had returned to the mainframe already, and was even now watching him through the station's sensors. Aidric would never again be able to reach out and touch her face or feel her breath on his neck as they lay together. He knew in his heart that her going back into the mainframe was best for everyone, even if he'd wanted her to stay.

He'd never wanted that level of devotion from anyone.

Even if it was something that he was willing to give to another.

Aidric knew his attention was split and it was important for him to focus on the matter at hand. "Garith, has security determined the best spots to monitor the crowd, while staying as inconspicuous as possible? With the number of diplomats present, I don't want to take any risks but nor do I want to give the impression that we don't trust one another."

"I'll have four teams stationed in and around the atrium." He moved toward Aidric with a data pad in hand. "This will give us the best protection without alarming anyone."

Aidric glanced down at the data pad, which was why he'd initially missed the commotion in the back of the atrium. When the shouting started, he immediately snapped his gaze to the back of the room. "What's happening?"

Taking a step toward the commotion, he stopped short when he realized who was at the center of everything. "Peri?"

"I thought she was – " Rykal shook his head. "She's with Darrick."

"What's the meaning of all this?" Yannis was standing behind Garith, no doubt prepared to use the security officer as a shield if need be. "That is a diplomat with the Callidon delegation."

"Everything's fine." Darrick had pushed the delegate to the floor and Aidric though he saw Darrick pulling what appeared to be a blaster from the diplomat's waistband. "We'd learned of a threat to the unification ceremony and it appears that the delegate is involved."

"Why wasn't I informed?" Garith's annoyance was clear.

"We weren't sure who was involved and wanted to keep the information contained." Aidric handed the data pad back to Garith. "Rykal."

"I'm on it."

As much as Aidric wanted to run over to Peri, he knew it would cause more harm than it would solve. He needed to wrap the mantle of commander around himself, to ensure no one saw him as anything less than the calm, controlled force who'd kept Grus Prime running and safe for half a century.

Even if he no longer wanted that.

Even if all he wanted was Peri.

The crowd parted and the Callidon diplomat glared at Peri. "What are you doing? What did they do to you?"

It was then that Aidric realized she hadn't put the lenses back in and the glow from the cybernetic matrix was visible in her eyes. There was no hiding the fact that she'd been reborn, or concealing that they're had been a previously unknown, still functioning matrix. He stepped forward, only to have Yannis move into his field of vision. "What did you do?"

"Nothing." He knew the truth didn't really matter to Yannis, just as it wouldn't to the high council. Peri's very existence put everything at risk. "She did this on her own."

"That's not possible. Someone living must implant the matrix and you've been forbidden to create another one."

"It was a prototype that I'd forgotten about. She hadn't."

Yannis grabbed his arm. "Who is *she*?"

She was one of the most important people in Aidric's life. "Her name is Peri."

Aidric stepped past Yannis, ignoring every claxon exploding in his brain warning him that he was putting everything he'd worked for at risk, simply by walking across the atrium to go to her. He didn't care. What good was living a life if he spent all his time alone, with no one to share in the joy of every day. He'd been selfish once, brought his brother back from the dead to help win a war, and had paid the price of solitude ever since. He'd convinced himself that he'd deserved this punishment, even though his actions had helped save his people. The dead hadn't asked to be reborn, nor asked to be shunned once they'd done the impossible and beat back the Sholle. That was on him and he'd accepted that responsibility.

But if Rykal had found it in his heart to forgive him, perhaps Aidric could forgive himself.

He cleared his throat and looked hard at the Callidon diplomat. It made little sense why someone of his status would want to try and derail the unification between the Grus and Fallen. Their people had been overrun with illicit and dark activities in their sector of space. Aidric had communications with the Empress herself about requesting help from the Grus once they actively reentered the political community of the quadrant. The Black Guard, a crime syndicate whose reach had far exceeded

Aidric's understanding had begun to infiltrate lower levels of politics on Callidon.

Cocking his head, Aidric narrowed his gaze on the diplomat. "You're not who was originally supposed to attend the ceremony from your planet."

"Aidric, get back to the dais where Garith can protect you." Rykal's tone was little more than a growl.

"Your name is Laban, isn't it?" Instead of listening, Aidric moved closer to him. "You're a low-level diplomat, if I recall. I find it difficult to believe that you'd be sent here for such an important event. The Grus and Fallen unification and our mutual reentry into the political landscape of this quadrant will be greatly beneficial to the Callidon people. Before our withdrawal, we ensured that certain criminal elements, say the Black Guard, were held in check."

Laban swallowed as he shifted his gaze away. "You don't know what you're talking about."

"Oh, I'm certain that I do." Aidric looked around at the crowd that had drawn near to watch the events unfolding. "There are many people who want to stop unification from happening. Do you know why?" He met the gaze of as many people as he could, wanting to know if they were even aware of their power. "Because the Grus are strong, we are just, and we take it upon ourselves to protect others. We'd forgotten that about ourselves for a long time. The wounds inflicted by the Sholle ran deep and we were scared. But we can't live in the shadows any longer. We can't leave groups like the Black Guard to continue to harm our neighbors."

The rumble of support for his words rolled through the crowd, growing in intensity as excitement built. This was the true beginning of unification, the people – his people – realizing that they didn't need to hide, that they could finally emerge and begin to live life once again with the others in this quadrant of space.

Aidric turned to look at Rykal, as his brother handed Laban over to one of the Grus security guards. When Rykal finally made eye contact with him, Aidric was shocked to see unshed tears illuminated by his glowing eyes. "Well, that was quite the speech."

There were so many things Aidric could say to him, but none of it truly mattered. Instead, he closed the distance between them and pulled his younger brother into a hug. "I would have burned down the galaxy to save you." He couldn't stop the sob, couldn't hold back the rush of fear and relief that escaped, instead he pressed his mouth to Rykal's shoulder to hide it. "Sorry."

Rykal squeezed him harder. "I forgive you. Never think that I haven't."

All the pain, the fear and tension that had lived within Aidric's entire being fell away, leaving him finally able to breathe.

It took a moment for him to collect himself, but as soon as he did, Aidric stepped away from Rykal and looked over at Peri. "Thank you."

Her eyes flashed as her mouth twitched into something that appeared to be a sad smile. "For you, anything. I'd do anything."

The crowd was chatting excitedly as Yannis approached them. "While this is all touching, you've still broken our laws, Commander Aidric. There was to have been no additional cybernetic matrixes left in existence after the war. You'd given us your solemn oath that this was truth. You have betrayed your people."

Yannis then pointed at Peri. "Garith, I want this cyborg detained and prepared for decommissioning."

"No!" Someone from the back of the crowd shouted. Others joined in, shouting their support. "Leave her alone!"

The entire atrium exploded into a flurry of activity and shouts, which was why Aidric hadn't realized that Laban had broken free from the security guard and now stood in the front of the crowd. Time slowed, as he watched Laban lift his arm and point a blaster at him. Aidric couldn't move, as though a tractor beam had somehow reached out and enveloped him, holding him fast. It was in that moment that he realized he might die.

There would be many regrets he'd have – taking Peri away from here, making love to her in the sunshine, waking up after a restful sleep with her in his arms – but if this was his end, he accepted it.

Shouts surrounded him as Laban fired and Aidric landed backward on the floor. But instead of the pain of a blaster shot, it was the solid weight of Peri on top of him, her body protecting his head and chest. "No, no, no, no." She pulled back to look down at him. "Are you hurt?"

Was he? "I don't think so."

Chaos was all around them, making it difficult for Aidric to know exactly what was going on, and despite his shoves against her, Peri wasn't moving. "Stay still."

"I need to – "

"Stay. Still."

Her additional strength from the nanobots and matrix made it impossible for him to overpower her, so all he could do was wait. Thankfully, it didn't take long for everything to settle down and Peri to slide off him, giving Aidric a glance at what had happened. Laban was pinned to the floor by several by-standers, the blaster gone from sight. What he hadn't expected was to see a second person also on the floor being held down by Darrick. "I saw him at the last second. Rykal?"

Rykal was also on the floor and moving to the side to reveal Yannis. "Are you harmed?"

"No." Yannis got to his feet as quickly as he was able, looking shocked. "But you appear to be."

Aidric moved to Rykal's side to check the blaster wound on his back. "You took the full force of it to your upper shoulder, but your nanobots are already effecting repair." Thank *frak*. "You might have reduced use of your arm for a few hours."

After the initial confusion resolved, Garith organized security forces to take Laban and the other would-be assassin into custody. Peri moved to Aidric's side, taking his hand in hers. "I guess he was Laban's backup plan if my attempt fell through."

"Let's hope they didn't have additional support."

Yannis cleared his throat. "Commander, you've managed to produce a second impossibility in your lifetime. I never thought our two peoples would ever come back together after the end of the Sholle war." He spoke loud enough that the crowd hushed.

"It wasn't all my doing, High Councillor. As you now see the Fallen and the Grus have always been and will forever be connected. We are one people."

Cheers erupted around them, and Peri gave his hand a squeeze.

Yes, there was one more thing that needed to be addressed. "I assume that given the circumstances, Peri's presence is no longer considered a threat. She did save my life, as Rykal has saved yours."

It was more than a little heavy handed on his part, but Aidric knew that the last thing Yannis would do in the current situation was to lose face or make a remark that could be used against the high council. Yannis lifted his chin and continued to look Aidric in the eyes. "I cannot pass judgment on her fate. However, I'll ensure the high council is aware of her actions here today."

The relief that washed through him was enough to buckle his knees. "Thank you."

Peri held him still. "While I appreciate everything, I think it's wise to escort Aidric to a safe location until the unification ceremony. We don't need to risk his life in the event of another attack."

Yannis gave them one final look before waving them away and turning his back on them to address Garith. Rykal and Darrick joined them, with Rykal cradling his wounded arm. "Let's get out of here."

Peri refused to let go of Aidric's arm even as they made their way through the crowd. "Do you want to go to your quarters? I only said that to get him away from us."

"No." He stopped and leaned down to kiss her hard on the mouth. "I thought I'd lost you. What happened?" She looked around at the group, but Aidric waved them away. "I thought you'd uploaded your code back into the mainframe?"

"I can't be certain, but it felt as though the mainframe wouldn't accept the changes to my AI code. Claimed that I was a virus and refused reintegration."

"That doesn't make sense. Even without your AI that code is adaptive and should have accepted you."

Peri bit her lower lip for a moment. "I think perhaps there was a part of it that realized I didn't want to return. That I wanted to stay here with you."

Aidric cupped her cheek, looking into those beautiful glowing eyes. "I'm so happy to hear that. Because I didn't want to lose you. I love you."

"I love you too." She hugged him hard and for once he felt as though everything would finally turn out for the best.

"What I want is for the two of us to crawl into bed and not get up until everything is over."

"I have a sneaking suspicion that won't happen." She kissed him once more. "Though once the ceremony is over, I plan to lock you in a room and kiss every inch of your body until you're begging to let you *frak* me."

He chuckled. "I like the sound of that."

"Excellent." She pulled away and they began to walk back toward where Rykal and Darrick stood waiting. "Then let's see this through to the end so we can get on with the rest of our lives."

Aidric smiled and finally knew in his heart that the universe had finally forgiven him.

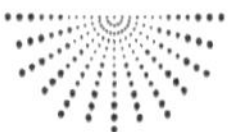

Peri couldn't help but to pace within the confines of Aidric's office, asked to wait there until the unification ceremony was complete. While there was still a threat that the Black Guard had managed to send in another operative, their plot had been exposed. Aidric was able to inform the other delegations of the threat, and the entirety of the visiting diplomatic envoys were on high alert. Aidric, Rykal, as well as everyone else were far safer now than they'd been even a few hours earlier.

That didn't mean Peri still didn't want to be there to ensure nothing bad happened to Aidric.

Computer, how much longer until the unification ceremony is complete? She looked up to the monitor, aware that the remaining AI was watching her.

The ceremony completed ten standard minutes ago.

Oh, Aidric should be on his way any moment. Then they would have to deal with the potential fallout of her actions. The high council had been made aware of her presence, where she'd come from and the status of Grus Prime's mainframe. While it appeared that the remnant code had enough of the original AI kernel that it continued to learn and adapt even after she'd downloaded herself into the matrix, Peri knew they still had concerns about how secure the station would be if she was unable to return.

There was a chance that they'd force Aidric to strip the personality elements she'd evolved into from her code and put the remainder back into the mainframe. Though he'd promised her that he'd never allow that to happen, she still couldn't help but worry that matters would quickly slip from their control.

She knew when Laban lifted the blaster and took aim at Aidric that she'd die for him. That had been so easy for her to commit to, didn't require much though at all. It had nothing to do with programming, coding that made her put his needs above all others. No, she loved him and that was the most important thing in the universe to her. But more importantly, she knew that he'd do the same for her. That if her life were ever in jeopardy, she knew in her heart that he'd sacrifice himself to save her.

That was true love.

Computer, is he on his way yet? She knew that even with the ceremony now over, he would need to speak with the diplomats, ensure that anyone who wanted a meeting with him to negotiate additional face time could do so. She knew it could still be hours before he'd arrive back in his office, and Peri was growing more and more selfish. She wanted him here with her so they could finally have a few moments of peace.

Commander Aidric and High Councillor Yannis are in the transportation tube and shall arrive in six point six minutes.

Peri froze. That wasn't a good sign. She looked down at this body that she'd taken not that long ago. The clothing still felt strange to put on every day and the rumble of her digestion system churning along to fuel her movements was far different from the code that encapsulated the entirety of her existence before now.

If Yannis was on the way, that meant the high council had reached a decision on her fate.

Running her hands through her hair and down her clothing, she did her best to look presentable. If her fate was sealed, the least she could do was face it with grace. The door chime sounded far sooner than she would have liked and sent a rush of adrenaline through her body. "Come in."

Yannis strode in first, his gaze snapping to her immediately, before he made his way to the center of the room and stood still. Aidric wasn't far behind him, but he didn't look her way. His face was blank, devoid of emotion, but she saw that there was something flickering in his gaze, even if he wouldn't look her in the eyes.

What the hell was happening?

Yannis sniffed loudly. "You've caused quite a few problems with your little…vacation."

Right, best to handle things directly. "Had I realized the difficulties my presence would have caused I would never have initiated the download."

"I find that hard to believe. Based on everything the commander here has told me, your actions were based on a flaw he'd inadvertently programmed into your code, making these events inevitable."

Peri chanced a glance at Aidric, surprised when she saw his gaze was now locked on her, his body relaxed even as Yannis approached her. "What does all of this mean?"

"It means that after we checked the mainframe and determined that the remaining AI is such that Grus Prime's security measures are still in place and shall keep us protected, we do not require your code to go back."

The tension in Peri's body was immediately sapped. "Oh. I can stay?"

"Yes, you can stay. However, there is still the matter of the crime that Commander Aidric has committed."

Aidric straightened. "What crime have I committed?"

"None of this would have happened if you hadn't retained a working cybernetic matrix. You'd told the council that all remaining working units had been destroyed after the war, that no other Fallen would ever be created. That the entirety of the process had been wiped away, never to be used again." Yannis turned to face him. "Not only did you lie to us, but you've also broken the law."

Peri's heart pounded harder at the thought of Aidric being punished for something that she'd done. "No, you can't blame him. He didn't know about the prototype. I'd made it appear that the matrix was gone, so I had the ability to use it one day."

"Peri." Aidric held out his arms and she immediately rushed to him, feeling a small measure of relief when he wrapped them around her body. "I should have destroyed it when I'd done so with the others. You might have concealed it from me, but I was the one who ensured it wasn't ruined in the first place."

Turning her face so she could look Yannis in the eyes, Peri braced herself for what was to come. "What is his punishment?"

Yannis held her gaze for a moment, no doubt wondering if she were about to lose control and rip his head off with the bad news he was about to relay. "After consultation with the council and the leader of the Fallen, the following has been decided. Aidric is herby stripped of his command and exiled from Grus Prime. All your research into the technology and code that created the Fallen that still remains is to be turned over to the high council where we will see to its destruction. The leader of the Fallen has agreed to allow both of you to live out your lives on the surface of Zarlan, though you will never again be allowed to return. Do you understand?"

A punishment indeed, and a harsh one for anyone other than Aidric.

They were going to get everything they ever wanted. She

turned her face and pressed it to his neck enjoying the rush of relief as it washed through her. "We can be together."

"Yes love. We can."

Yannis made his way toward the door. "You will of course need to wait until the delegations have returned to their planets. There's no reason to give anyone a reason to doubt the strength of our convictions to return to quadrant politics. But I expect you to have all your possessions on the last shuttle to Zarlan the moment the last diplomat has left."

"Understood, High Councillor."

"Thank you." Peri added, though far softer than Aidric.

Yannis looked at them both a moment longer, before nodding and stepping away, leaving them now finally alone. Peri closed her eyes and breathed in the scent of Aidric, no longer fearful that this might be the last time she'd have the chance. They stood there for a long time, wrapped in one another's arms, breathing. Knowing that they had the rest of their biological lives together was somehow both reassuring and overwhelming at the same time.

What would she do with her life? What kind of person would she become? Would Aidric be content to live a life on a planet that was still broken? Would he always love her the way she loved him?

"You're thinking very loudly." His words rumbled in his chest, sending pleasant vibrations through her.

"I was wondering if you'd always be happy with me, or if you'd regret being forced to live with me."

"I've lived most of my life alone. The thought of finally having someone to be with me, to share my thoughts and dreams with - it's more than I'd ever thought I deserved. But knowing that you're the person that I've been blessed with as a mate, I couldn't have asked for anything better."

Aidric turned her face with his finger and leaned down to kiss her soft, but intently. In that moment, Peri knew that the rest of their lives might not be perfect, but together, they'd be able to face anything.

"I love you," she whispered.

"I love you too." He kissed the tip of her nose.

"Let's start packing your things. I have a feeling that the council is going to make sure we're on that shuttle the moment the last diplomat leaves."

Aidric shrugged. "I have everything I need right here."

Peri smiled as the promise of the rest of their lives together stretched out before them.

ACKNOWLEDGMENTS

Thank you everyone for reading, SEDUCED BY THE CYBORG! Keep up to date with new releases, sales, and special information by joining my newsletter. Want to read the book that started it all? CONSUMED BY THE CYBORG is available now from Amazon and KU!

ALSO BY ALYSE ANDERS

Cyborg Protectors – Origins

Consumed by the Cyborg

Mated to the Cyborg

Saved by the Cyborg

Healed by the Cyborg

Cyborg Protectors – Prison

Chained to the Cyborg

Freed by the Cyborg

Exposed by the Cyborg

Redeemed by the Cyborg

Cyborg Rogues

Eion

Qwin

Weixler

Gadiel

ABOUT THE AUTHOR

Alyse Anders is the author of the Cyborg Protector series of erotic sci-fi novellas. When she's not sitting in front of her computer with her imagination stuck in a far away nebula, she's at home with her husband and two dogs, usually eating far too much chocolate for her own good. Check out more of Alyse's books on Amazon and KU or visit her website www.alyseanders.com.

www.ingramcontent.com/pod-product-compliance
Lightning Source LLC
Chambersburg PA
CBHW022101050726
47591CB00002B/626